The Devil's Reward

The Devil's Reward

Emmanuelle de Villepin

TRANSLATED FROM THE FRENCH
BY C. JON DELOGU

Other Press New York

Longanesi & C. © 2016 – Milano

Gruppo editoriale Mauri Spagnol

Originally published in Italian as *La parte del diavolo* in 2016 by Longanesi & C., Milan

English translation copyright © Other Press 2018

Text on pages 51–53 from https://en.wikipedia.org /wiki/Battle_of_the_Somme; this work is reproduced under the Creative Commons Attribution-ShareAlike license, https:// en.wikisource.org/wiki/Creative_Commons_Attribution-ShareAlike_2.0

Rudolf Steiner quote on pages 172–173 from http://wn.rsarchive.org /Books/GA026/ English/APC1956/GA026_c29.html

Production editor: Yvonne E. Cárdenas

Text designer: Julie Fry

This book was set in Fournier with Parma Petit by Alpha Design & Composition of Pittsfield, NH

10 9 8 7 6 5 4 3 2 1

Library of Congress Cataloging-in-Publication Data

Names: De Villepin, Emmanuelle, 1959- author. | Delogu, Christopher Jon, translator.
Title: The devil's reward : a novel / Emmanuelle de Villepin ; translated from the French by Christopher Jon Delogu.
Other titles: Parte del diavolo. English
Description: New York : Other Press, 2018. | "Originally published in Italian as La parte del diavolo in 2016 by Longanesi & C., Milan" — Verso title page. | An English translation of an unpublished French translation of the original Italian edition.
Identifiers: LCCN 2017028619 | ISBN 9781590518687 (paperback) | ISBN 9781590518694 (ebook)
Subjects: LCSH: Mothers and daughters—Fiction. | Grandmothers—Fiction. | Families—Fiction. | Marriage—Fiction. | Adultery—Fiction. | Life change events—Fiction. | Europe—Fiction. | Domestic fiction. | BISAC: FICTION / Family Life. | FICTION / Contemporary Women. | FICTION / Historical.
Classification: LCC PQ4904.E33 P3713 2018 | DDC 853/.92—dc23 LC record available at https://lccn.loc.gov/2017028619

To my mother

"Go, I don't know where, bring back I don't know what. The way is long and the path is unknown."

(from a Russian tale)

Chapter One

When I got back from running errands that morning, I went to lie down on my bed because I was feeling a little short of breath. I wasn't hungry. My fish seller had let me eat a lot of shrimp, which I love, and I also couldn't resist munching nearly half of my warm baguette as I walked along rue Madame on the way back to my home on Place Saint-Sulpice. I picked up the TV remote and switched it on as I always do, because although I like to be alone, I hate silence. The television—always on—is like a spirit or ceiling fan in my big apartment. It was already big when my husband was alive. Today it seems enormous—a continent with threatening areas, forests of memories, and a bay of solitude. I haven't changed a thing. The wallpaper and everything else is the same. His clothes are still hanging in the armoire, and I still have the silent expectation of hearing his key in the door. I've done everything I can to get used to it, but with no success. That's what comes with old age—the loss of resilience. When something breaks, one is pulled down into a bottomless pit with no chance of one day recovering from losses. A really good film, *The Lady from Shanghai*, was on. In the climax, Rita Hayworth is caught in a shoot-out in a hall of mirrors at a fair. She is stunningly beautiful, her image is multiplied to infinity by the mirrors, and shots shatter her reflection several times. Dozens of Rita Hayworths make the same gestures and have the same frightened look, while all the faces of the killer seem to be saying, as the noise of glass and guns rings out, "Damn, which one is *her*?"

The telephone rang. It was my daughter. She lives in Italy with her Milanese husband. She was sobbing because she had discovered that her husband was cheating on her... again. She gets worked up about it every time, and every time I'm tempted to say things to her that I think I would regret later. I suggested she come and spend a few days with me in Paris, the city of her childhood. She accepted. I'm a little ashamed, however, because even though my daughter's pain should be uppermost in my mind, I'm mostly pleased at the prospect of her coming. A mother's narcissism is complicated, tangled, opaque, and difficult to understand because always intermixed with love, ideas of sacrifice, and feelings of guilt. But perhaps I'm exaggerating and, mother or not, a portion of egocentrism is simply a part of us all. So to hell with my reservations—I would have Catherine all to myself and enjoy it! Besides, I would finally feel useful. One can't deny that old ladies like myself have tons of experience. When things are going to hell, we at least have this advantage: we know the truth—everything always ends badly.

I started thinking of everything I would prepare for her —her favorite meals, outings, and so on. Madame Joseph, my cleaning lady who also does some ironing for me, stuck her head around the door of my bedroom and I recited a list of things to do in preparation for my daughter's visit. The telephone rang again and it was again Catherine. She told me she would be arriving the next morning and with my granddaughter Luna too. Now this is awful to say, but I couldn't care less anymore about the hanky-panky that my son-in-law was indulging in with some birdbrain, because I was over the moon. I tried not to let on too much, but my smart daughter noticed my joy and was irritated. Too bad. They were coming the next day and I was delighted.

I got up to see if their bedrooms were all ready. Passing by my husband's study, I closed my eyes. I do that every time I go by so as not to see he's missing—it helps a little. I've told Madame Joseph not to open the doors to the library so that it retains the odor of his cigars. Unfortunately, as time goes by the smell evaporates. I fear the day when I won't smell anything anymore.

The beds needed to be made, but Madame Joseph would get that done while I went out to buy pink tulips for Luna and white roses for Catherine. They would match the wallpaper, plus they're my favorite colors.

When I got back I decided to take a short nap. I fell asleep and had a dream, which is very unusual for me these days. I found myself in a forest of mirrors that reflected my image. They were all me but at different ages. Someone was shooting at me—I don't know who or why—and my image broke into thousands of shards that the other versions of me contemplated, looking bewildered and absorbed.

Chapter Two

I was watching Luna as she devoured a chocolate éclair while reading a book by Rudolf Steiner. Now and then she would push her blond curls away from her face with her wrist while her two hands were busy holding her fork and the book. She was really lovely. She got her big dark eyes and blond hair from her mother, from her father she inherited a beautiful full mouth and big sparkly teeth.

"You're interested in Steiner?"

"Why, do you know him?"

"My father met him but my aunt Bette knew him well. She even spent quite a bit of time at his home in Dornach, near Basel. You know, at that place—what was it called?"

"You mean the Goetheanum?"

"Yes, exactly, at the Goetheanum."

"That's incredible! I'm writing a thesis about Steiner and my great-grandfather actually knew him—that's amazing!"

"Yes, truly amazing. So what's your thesis about?"

"It's entitled 'Mediating Challenges'—I'm trying to explain why and how certain features of Steiner's pedagogical system ought to be applied in non-Steiner schools."

"And you really believe that?"

"Absolutely." Proud to show off her knowledge, Luna continued, "Our whole school system is totally a product of Piaget's thinking, with all the steps to be mastered, grading, and competitiveness. Steiner introduced a mediating instance between the curriculum to be followed and the capacities of the child. For him, the teacher must exercise intuition and draw out the student without creating a continuous state of frustration if he does not understand something as quickly as others of his age. Not to mention children with learning disabilities! With Steiner there's really attention to other aspects of human development — creativity, feelings, and individual will. It's super important, don't you think?"

"You obviously know a lot about these questions — I'm very impressed! I always considered Steiner to be a sympathetic light keeper. But really all that I know came down to me from stories told by Aunt Bette and Papyrus. She was a total convert, whereas he was very opposed."

"They told you things about him?"

"Of course, thousands of times!"

Catherine suddenly appeared in the dining room, her eyes red, and slumped down into one of the chairs. "Watch out, honey — your grandmother has always been quite the storyteller! You need to take everything she says with a grain of salt. We just finished lunch and you're already snacking? Really, you never stop eating!"

She really has a knack for ruining everything. It would be no exaggeration to say she's a real sourpuss. I make up stories, I make too much for lunch, and — horrors! — I light a cigarette at the end of the meal. For over fifty years I've been smoking two cigarettes a day under the wrathful gaze of my busybody daughter.

"When you act like that, you put me in the mood for a double scotch! Oh, five o'clock already! Would you also like a double scotch, Luna dear?"

My granddaughter flashes me her big smile while Catherine tosses me a sad look.

"I'm just kidding," I say to her, a bit irritated.

"I know, but how do you do it?" says Catherine. "I'd give anything to have your lightness of being for even a minute."

"It's not simply a gift, my girl. It's daily training and iron discipline, you know."

"Me, I have no sense of humor."

"Yes you do, Mom," says Luna kindly. "You make me laugh sometimes."

"Okay, and so who is this Steiner?"

"A philosopher. An Austrian intellectual who studied pedagogy. Did you know there are more than eight hundred Steiner schools around the world? But he also got involved in architecture, medicine, art, esotericism, and agriculture. For example, he invented biodynamic agriculture, such as with the Weleda products. And he's noted for being the founder of anthroposophy."

"Never heard of him."

"But Catherine, don't you remember my aunt Bette?"

"Of course I do."

"Well, she talked about him nonstop."

"I have no recollection of that. What did he found?"

"Weleda. You remember all those products you used when Luna was a baby?"

"Oh yes, true. I remember now. My pediatrician was always recommending that stuff. But what was that other thing you mentioned?"

"Anthroposophy?"

"Right! Mom, do you know what that is?" asked Catherine.

"Vaguely. It is a less orientalist version of theosophy, isn't that right, Luna?"

"But what is theosophy? I don't understand a thing you're saying!"

"Ah, you remind me of my brother Gabriel and me when we were little. All those words were so obscure for us that we'd throw them at each other's faces like fistfuls of sand!"

"Okay, and so what is theosophy?"

"Briefly put," Luna explained, "it's an esoteric school founded by Helena Blavatsky that focuses on a comparative analysis of religions, sciences, and philosophies, and tries to rediscover man's latent capacities."

"And Steiner was a theosophist?"

"At the beginning, yes, but then he distanced himself from it to found his anthroposophy."

"And what's the difference?"

"Fundamentally I would say it turns on the role of Christ."

"But all this attention to the spiritual world, isn't it a bit in contradiction with Catholicism?" I asked.

"Steiner totally refuted the dogmas of the church, but he considered Jesus as the only incarnation of spirit capable of getting beyond the scientific materialism of the West. This was the total opposite of Madame Blavatsky, and after her death Annie Besant. They were only interested in Eastern philosophies."

"My daughter certainly knows a lot! But you, Mom, did you really know all that or are you bluffing? It's all totally beyond me, I can tell you that."

Catherine is beautiful, there's no doubt about that. It's perhaps because I made her, but everyone always used to tell me how stunning she looked. She just thickened up a bit these past years, probably eating too much. Her problem—and I say this out of immense love for her—is that she's very tiresome. She got that from my mother. Everything is a big deal to her. She is constantly on the lookout, nostrils dilated sniffing every danger, ears cocked to detect the slightest threat. Her husband grants himself a few too many liberties, but they've been married for thirty-odd years and she spends her life spying on him. It's as though all these tragedies that she's staging were giving her a reason to live. If she knew that I cheated on her father and how much he cheated on me she'd hit the ceiling. And yet we loved each other. None of our lovers were ever of any real importance, but that was another time. People tended to marry only once and they easily got used to the idea of having later on a sort of fraternal friend with whom to finish out one's days. In between, people occupied themselves as best they could, but we had enough sense not to confuse everything. At least in our families it was like that.

For my daughter, on the other hand, it's a tragedy. She always had a tendency to dramatize things, but in this my little girl is powerless, it's just the way she is. And obviously it's not for me, her mother, to tell her to take a lover of her own. It always pains me to hear her go on like this. Really, why does she obsess about snooping into her husband's business? No couple can withstand such up-close inspection. Despite having passed the fifty-year milestone, my daughter is totally lacking in wisdom and discernment. I told her to come to my home immediately, without going into explanations, so that she'd build a little mystery around herself too. After all, one has the right to defend one's dignity! Being serially betrayed is not doing anything for her self-esteem or "wellness," as people say now. Even I was a bit shaken by it. I placed my hand on her cheek.

"You've been crying again, my dear, perhaps we should have a talk."

"I have nothing to say. You know very well what's going on but you don't understand it completely."

She was not wrong about that, though I do remember having been quite jealous myself. The difference is my life was very full and I never liked to suffer. It also must be said from the summit of my eighty-six years, and so I'll say it, my relationship was a marvelous love story that no assortment of petty interferences ever stained. If Catherine knew what I would give to be in her place — having only to dial a number to speak with him, even if it's just to hear a pack of lies. When they lie to us, it means they still love us. That's another feature of these modern times — this obsession with clarity and truth. I find that presumptuous and unaesthetic. The presumption comes from the arrogance of these sincere types who insist on saying everything that's on their mind even if it's not required. They might as well burp in people's faces, it would have about the same effect. It is unaesthetic because the tumult of our feelings and contradictions is like the growling of our stomachs, which it is rather indelicate to inflict on others. Just as the water closet was invented, so was the secret, and that worked just fine. Today, however, everyone knows everything about everybody, and the rule has become to always tell the truth. The result is a world of voyeurs and masochists, for whom love must produce the same effect as the two fangs of Dracula planted in the jugular.

Coming back to my daughter, she breaks my heart. It's like watching a kitten parachuted into a war zone. She lacks the necessary sense of humor and solid regard for herself, and for facing up to life that's like going to war with no ammunition and no bulletproof vest.

She threw me a quick glance and rested her head on my shoulder sobbing. Luna was chewing slowly, watching her and feeling uncomfortable about how much pleasure she was having while her mother was suffering.

"Does it really hurt that much, my dear?"

"Oh Mother, you can't imagine how it burns into me. You have no idea. Papa always adored you."

"But Lorenzo too would never want to lose you."

"Well, then why have we had all these conflicts?"

"Don't you think you're exaggerating a bit? Your 'conflicts' never really threatened you."

"Oh really? How do you know?"

"You always ended up making peace."

"Not this time."

"Why? What's so different this time?"

"I hate myself."

"But you've done nothing wrong, my darling."

"If only she'd done something wrong!" interjected Luna. I love that child!

"Your daughter is right. Your problem is that you over-value the marriage pact. You give it supreme authority. You don't take nature into account. Desire has a way of not always harmonizing with constancy and good habits. Desire is the son of the goddess Penia, who wanders about famished. Do you remember your Plato? Desire needs a lack, love is something else again. Love is just the opposite."

"But Mother, what are you talking about? Love and desire are inseparable!"

"Desire can very well run on its own steam, I guarantee you. Have you never desired another man?"

"No."

"Mom, be honest," said Luna, wide-eyed.

"Well, not too much."

"Tell us if you ever wanted to be with another man. Just like that, out of pure curiosity."

"Wanted, wanted...no. At any rate, not enough to cheat."

"So you've never cheated on Lorenzo? Not even in your thoughts?"

"No."

"Well, my dear, this is terrible news you're sharing with me."

"But Mom!"

"But Grandma!"

"Discovering at my age that my only daughter is a victim — I assure you this is a terrible shock!" I always have to lay it on thick to get others to look beyond the ugliness of old age. I choose to be resolutely nonconformist and scandalous. I hate those qualities in young people, but I find them charming among us oldsters, and I would sell my soul to be viewed sympathetically by these two women.

"But Mom, sex is not the only thing in life! You really amaze me. I lived for my family, my home, our trips, our relations — for all the things that make decent people tranquil and happy, is that so awful?"

"Okay, but amid all that order and perfection, you were missing something fundamental."

"Oh really, what?"

"The devil's reward. All this goodness and wellness and appropriateness is as dangerous as their opposites. Believe me, my girl, I've had plenty of time to measure what one owes to the sacred and what must not under any circumstances be denied to the profane."

Chapter Three

We were coming back from a long outing at the Jardin des Plantes. Luna had developed a singular affection for a pair of red pandas. We walked slowly as I like to do, observing everything with our full attention. What I like about my granddaughter is that she's always looking for a new angle. She likes looking at things from on high, from below, and from all sides, front and back. She also stopped several times to look up at the sky. It's very pretty to observe her long neck tilt back and see her cascade of blond curly hair fall lower down her back. Poor Catherine would not stop sighing. I've always had the habit of simplifying and seeking out the humorous side of things, but it does not protect me much from all that's sad.

During the walk Luna spoke more about her thesis on Steiner and said again how astonished she was to learn that my father had known him.

"Hmm, you mean I've never spoken to you about my father?"

"No. Is he the man on the horse next to your bed?"

"Yes, he was an excellent rider. He attended Saint-Cyr."

"What was his name again?"

"Louis, but my brother and I called him Papyrus."

"You loved him, didn't you?"

"I adored him, but it was a real disaster."

"Really? Why?"

"Oh, it's a long story."

"And your mother?"

"A perfect woman."

"Terrible you mean?"

"Inoffensive but unbearable all the same."

"You didn't love her?"

"Of course I did! We didn't get along, but that's another matter."

"And what did you know about Papyrus and Steiner? And no making stuff up, I need solid material!"

"But I don't need to invent anything! It bothers me when you and your mother accuse me of that. A story, even about historical events, remains a story, you know. Would you ask a master chef to cook without salt?"

"*Oh là là*, you certainly have a high opinion of your story-telling skills."

"True, but also for what I lived through. So I'm going to tell you things as I lived them and not as though it were the evening news, got it?"

She laughed and I did too.

We had hardly stepped in the door when Madame Joseph rushed up, her cheeks on fire, visibly thrilled at being dragged into the family drama. She told us that Lorenzo had called several times and insisted each time on how important it was for Catherine to contact him. My daughter made no reply and went to her room. I contemplated consoling her, but she said she preferred to be alone. I had to pass by my husband's office to get to the kitchen to prepare tea. Luna was reading. It was so sweet to have the two women in my life all to myself, a pot of Lapsang souchong steeping, and to recollect our magnificent walk in the Jardin des Plantes, but Catherine's suffering prevented the light from shining forth completely. That was life—constantly moving among obstacles to reach its fruits.

In a closet there was a large military trunk in which I saved everything to do with my father. I was the only survivor of my family.

I had not opened that big green metal trunk in ages, and now suddenly I was experiencing weird feelings about this ancient storage box of mine. I was accustomed to its presence but I remembered nothing about what was inside it. It had two rusty latches and an open padlock hung from the left one. I removed it, and with the uneasy feeling that I was opening a casket, I grabbed the two upper pieces of each latch and tried to lift the lid. It didn't budge. I tried several times with all of my senior citizen strength, but it was no use, the trunk refused to open.

Catherine appeared in the doorway.

"Mother, what are you doing?"

"I'm trying to open Papyrus's trunk."

She had a go at it, first alone and then with my help. Finally the lid came up and a cloud of dust made us cough. Peering into my father's trunk hardly revealed a pot of gold. With my thumb and index finger I picked up the gray rag that I supposed was what remained of his hussar's military coat. I avoided shaking it and placed it delicately on some boxes stacked nearby. The things it had been covering were in better condition: books, notepads, various objects, pipes, a small silver ball for storing opium, and a framed saint's medal pierced by a bullet mounted on a plum-colored piece of velvet.

"What's that?" asked Catherine.

"A miracle. My mother ceremoniously gave him a necklace with this medallion of the Virgin to wear as he set off to war, and can you believe it, that atheist had his life saved by that present. See for yourself."

Catherine dusted off the frame and stared at it.

"Wow, incredible," she said without lifting her eyes.

Her hands were covered with freckles and her nails, curved and healthy, struck me tenderly all of a sudden. As a young girl, Catherine already had the hands of an adult. I remember her clutching her baby bottle with the fingers of a miniature woman. In fact she always gave me the impression of having a spirit that was older than her years. At a time when the world ought to have hit her with its banal materiality, when all children have their eyes lit up by every little conquest, Catherine behaved like a grand bourgeoise who was above such things.

"You said it! To think that my mother's faith ended up saving his life."

Chapter Four

It was a very long time ago, so far back that my memory and my imagination have gotten mixed up in the story I'm about to tell. This story has a historic basis for me alone, and the only thing that matters to me is to relate what I experienced — there's nothing objective about it. In fact, even in History with a capital *H* there's nothing impartial. All that counts really are the traces that events have imprinted on our lives and those can only be communicated in one's own particular way. I'm the only one who can tell you what happened to me, and I will tell it to you without hypocrisy or trickery. I'm not a liar, I'm a storyteller, and since I'm talking about my life, I would like to be trusted.

I must have been five or six, maybe seven or even eight, it doesn't matter. I was a child, of that I'm certain, because I still had intact the capacity to fully give myself up body and soul to the joys of life with the illusion that everything life offered needed to be seized gluttonously. It was Easter Sunday. On the order of my father, my brother, my mother, and I were looking out the tall windows of the living room to see signs of winter retreating slowly like a wolf. Between patches of old snow that still covered the lawn a few crocuses were beginning to come up. At the far end of the yard one could clearly see the orderly row of plane trees that bordered the allée leading to the main gate. The leafless rosebushes still looked like naked porcupines and the large potted hydrangea plants on either side of the entryway also looked rather sad. The stone bust of the pretty woman was covered with leaves, as though to protect her from hoarfrost. She looked rather fragile and miserably immobile in this setting of interminable waiting and expectations. Buds on the willow branches, a hint of new green in the brownish snow-damaged lawn, and a female blackbird frantically building her nest were lighter promises of better days to come. I always felt inside the cheerfulness of spring resonating like a harbinger telling of future surprises.

The car of Uncle Geoffroy and Aunt Bette glided between the plane trees, followed next by the car of Cousin Vincent and his wife Elodie. Aunt Bette was the widow of my mother's brother, Uncle Enguerrand, who had died in the First World War. She later married the brother of Papyrus. Our mother didn't care much for this double sister-in-law, whom she considered aloof, but Bette paid no mind and got along fine with the men in the family.

The joyful party entered the living room chatting gaily and I detected a whiff of excitement around my mother, even though she greeted each one in the group with the doleful reserve that was her way.

My brother Gabriel, two years older than me, had climbed atop a Louis XV trumeau, and though our mother insisted he get down immediately, he wiggled up there and made faces that caused me to burst out laughing.

"You little imp, come down from there this instant! You're going to break your neck!" insisted our mother at the very moment Papyrus, looking disheveled, entered the room.

He gave an amused glance in the direction of my brother, which singularly annoyed my mother.

"Oh, Louis, say something! He's going to fall and hurt himself!"

"Fly into my arms, my angel Gabriel, I will catch you in flight."

My fearless brother did not need to be asked twice before launching himself toward my father, who broke his fall as they both fell to the floor with laughter that spread to everyone in the group except to my aggrieved mother. Our hilarity isolated her and further confirmed her role as the killjoy of the family. Papyrus and Gabriel rolled on the floor indifferent to her pinched stares. She then started for the door.

"Marguerite, where are you going?" asked my father out of breath.

"I'm leaving you to your fun."

"Oh come on, don't take it like that! Go to the window, all of you, and wait for me. The Easter bells seem to be on their way."

"On their way where? Where, Papyrus?" yammered my brother.

"On their way here. Go to the window. I'm going to get something and I'll be back. Wait for me and don't budge."

Aunt Bette and Uncle Geoffroy exchanged looks that I didn't know how to interpret but that I remember to this day. We did exactly what Papyrus told us to do. I was standing between Aunt Bette and my brother when the bells started ringing—at first far off and gradually closer until they became deafening. Magnificent bells of every color rose and fell before our wondering eyes. We'd paid no attention to Papyrus's absence as he now returned on tiptoe and witnessed our continued amazement at this whole production without either my brother or me realizing that he had engineered the whole thing. We were all worked up and continued to gaze at the horizon in the hope that some slowpoke bells were yet to arrive.

The family then filed off to the castle chapel, where the parish priest officiated at a mass for the whole village. On the way, my mother held a handkerchief over her face to prevent any grains of dust from fouling her mouth, which was about to receive the body of Christ. Since we were still laughing, she complained and ordered us to close our mouths with the aim of a similar Christian hygiene. But her scolding orders which sought to gag us only redoubled our laughter. Poor Mother—if only all her obsessions had helped her to be less unhappy. Aunt Bette held us by the hand smiling. The three men followed a few steps behind, speaking of things that did not interest me.

Gabriel and I were only invited to the grown-ups' dinner table at major holidays. We were always happy on those occasions but would end up being horribly bored. We came to the table in our squeaky-clean Sunday clothes and were invariably welcomed by the angry stares of our mother, who could not bear a badly tied ribbon or an errant lock of hair. Once seated, we were forbidden to speak unless spoken to. The worst was that these meals went on forever. In fact they constituted my first experience of desire and the concomitant disappointment at its not being fulfilled. Gabriel would later call this form of emptiness after exaltation the *post coitum* sadness—but at the time we were too young to use such language.

If I'm talking about this memorable Easter Sunday meal, it's because it was then that I first heard the name Rudolf Steiner and because it would seem that some family secret was inseparably linked to it.

"So Bette, how did you find the new Goetheanum?"

"Much less handsome than the former. The first was nicely round and welcoming, whereas the second appears to be on the defensive. It's as though after the fire Rudolf wanted to ensure the safety of anthroposophy. It looks like an enormous concrete beetle, and yet there's a spiritual atmosphere that's reassuring if one's mind doesn't wander too much."

"Did you see any interesting dance or theater?"

"Of course, I saw the entire four-play cycle, and Marie Steiner von Sivers informed me that she was working on staging a complete *Faust*."

"And are they still performing demonstrations of eurythmy?"

"Nothing's changed. Well, I suppose things have evolved a little bit, but always in the spirit of Steiner."

This exchange took place between Aunt Bette and my father. My mother looked exasperated but Cousin Vincent and Uncle Geoffroy were listening attentively. Aunt Elodie was eating with gusto and paying no mind to the conversation around her. She raised her chin now and then and smiled nicely in a way that made adorable dimples appear on her pink cheeks.

What distinguished Bette from other women of her day was not simply her modern and sensual beauty. She was intelligent and knew all sorts of things that country squires in our neighborhood knew nothing about. She had grown up in a rich family in Basel and had met my mother's brother at a ball in Paris. It was love at first sight. My mother's family was not enthused, however, because Bette had absolutely no social rank. She was Swiss and her international manners probably frightened the local hicks in our area. She became a widow at a young age and then remarried Uncle Geoffroy, but she maintained total independence, traipsing wherever she liked. My mother, who loved but never understood her brother, also never accepted his widow's unbridled ways. So much freedom unnerved and upset her. It should be added that Aunt Bette knew how to pour it on, and all the men in the family were spellbound. My mother had no notions about anything that had been said. She remarked only one thing: Bette traveled alone and that ought to have been considered scandalous instead of admired.

The discussion of the Goetheanum continued. This was the center for anthroposophy built by Steiner and ostentatiously named to honor Goethe, whose writings Steiner took as the main inspiration for his own thinking. Aunt Bette often spoke of Rudolf Steiner, Marie von Sivers, and eurythmy—and these new words had a sort of comic ring to our ears. Gabriel made a face every time one of our table guests uttered the words Steiner, Goetheanum, or eurythmy, and the grown-ups' obliviousness of us made him bolder each time. It was all I could do not to burst out laughing. My mother noticed our antics and shot us a quick admonishing stare. She detested this topic of conversation and felt excluded, so she played her parental role but without conviction. After swallowing the last morsel of dessert, we were allowed to leave the table and did so quickly and noisily.

At the time of my birth, Papyrus had someone carve a baptismal font in the trunk of an ancient oak, and it was in the hollow of that large mass of wood that my baptism was celebrated. Gabriel and I used to run there and sit down panting and then discuss all that we'd heard and seen. That day I tripped him and he fell flat on his face and scraped his knee. He said it stung a bit. When I bent down to blow on it—imitating what the grown-ups did when we hurt ourselves—he slapped me hard. In tears, I slapped him back and we ended up fighting like two stray cats. When I finally pleaded with him to stop because he was hurting me, Gabriel stood up, threw a fistful of my hair at me, and said, "Scram, you dumb Rudolfsteiner!"

"I'm not talking to you anymore, you dumb Goetheanum!" I shot back.

"Get out of my sight and go cry in your corner!"

Which is what I did.

The men were smoking fat cigars while my mother and Aunt Bette played cards in her private sitting room, where a nice fire crackled in the fireplace. I slipped up the stairs unnoticed and ran to my bedroom. A short time later Gabriel knocked on my door. The bogey brother was bored.

"Hey, it's Goetheanum, will you open up?"

"If you think you're funny, think again."

"I know I'm funny, now open up!"

I opened the door. Staring at my torn dress and mussed-up hair, he started laughing. He then got the idea of having me make an appearance in our mother's sitting room. I always did what Gabriel told me to do. He was quite a sight too, with his soiled shorts and bloody knee. And so it was in that state that we burst in on Aunt Bette, Elodie, and my mother, shouting "Coal delivery!" and laughing hysterically as they looked on horrified. The three men were laughing too, which encouraged us further despite my mother's crestfallen look. The poor woman—she really deserved better than us two little savages.

That evening my parents hosted a reception to celebrate Easter, and rooms were prepared for Uncle Geoffroy, Aunt Bette, Cousin Vincent, and Aunt Elodie to stay the night. Dinner parties like these were for us a real treat. We could eat delicious little things without having to sit at the table, we could hide at the top of the stairs and watch guests arrive without being seen, and we could criticize everyone and analyze every detail. It was like going to the movies.

Aunt Bette came up from behind and surprised us, patting our heads in a friendly gesture. She was magnificent in her long red dress, and I knew already that it was going to annoy my mother. She was always charming with us and yet we didn't like her much. I don't know how to explain it, but her every word and movement had something haughty about it that was exasperating to us rascals. Thinking back on it, I'm still surprised how much ascendancy she had over the men in my family. All three were crusty, impenitent cavalrymen, and their interest in her and her theories was probably based more on a primitive attraction for her physique than any real philosophical convictions. Although…

Everything started at the end of the First World War when Papyrus had been lightly wounded in combat, Vincent and Geoffroy survived the trenches, and Bette, newly widowed, took up spiritualism and a relatively new school of thought disseminated by a certain Rudolf Steiner: anthroposophy. My mother was only a girl then, ten years younger than my father, who would gallop under the windows of the boarding school for girls she attended, either alone or with other riders. They had fun performing acrobatic feats to this audience of wide-eyed virgins. My father met my mother at some ball in the area. She had grace and was of a good family but far too young for him to take notice of. Vincent, Geoffroy, and Louis were famous throughout the land for liking the ladies. Their high jinks were notorious, but they were considered charming, funny, worthy gentlemen.

When war erupted, the three hardy fellows, who were enrolled at the military academy Saint-Cyr, were called into combat. My grandfather organized a ball in their honor, and among the guests was the woman who would become my mother. She was a child and nothing happened between them, but she found the courage, most likely with cheeks flushed and legs trembling, to approach and bestow on him a silver medal of the Virgin, saying that it would protect him. And the rogue put it around his neck.

Chapter Five

E nguerrand was the same age as Papyrus and they were quite close. After meeting Bette he distanced himself from his friends and lived only for her. All that romance lasted only a short while, however, because the war started a few months after their wedding. Each time he returned from the front they would shut themselves in their bedroom and only emerge at mealtimes. Theirs was an all-consuming passion, and it's not impossible that this contributed to the scant sympathy my mother had for her sister-in-law.

It was then that Bette met a certain Jeanne de Valcourt, who hosted Spiritism sessions for friends and acquaintances several times a week. At first there were only a few individuals of the upper bourgeoisie who attended, but as news from the front slowed to a trickle, many people asked her for help in contacting the dead and inquired about the fate of their relatives in the trenches. Aunt Bette was most impressed by the first meeting she attended. She claimed the pedestal table used by Jeanne rose off the floor and started spinning like a top—leaving everyone present terrorized. Bette had no trouble being persuaded that the medium had disturbed some spirits who then took revenge on her with this trick. It left her so frightened she promised never to return. And yet another event, more dramatic still, convinced her forever that life after death was real.

Enguerrand died from wounds caused by a bomb that exploded a few hours before the Armistice was signed. Aunt Bette was reading by the fire that November morning when she saw the door open and Enguerrand appeared before her. She knew immediately that something terrible had happened.

"Enguerrand, is that you?" she asked without getting an answer.

She did not throw her arms around his neck as she would usually have done, because she sensed this was a paranormal appearance. Her husband was dead, she just knew it. After caressing her with terribly sad eyes, Enguerrand turned, went out the door, and disappeared forever.

When she was informed of the death of her husband, Aunt Bette had already been in mourning for several days, though without confiding in anyone about the strange apparition. She feared that she would be accused of making the whole thing up, but in truth that strange experience left her feeling anxious and sad.

She then decided to go to Basel and spend several days with her family.

In Basel, Aunt Bette reunited with her older sister Greta, who after her own husband's death had come back to live in the family home on the banks of the Rhine. Bette's father owned a pharmaceutical business and had raised everyone to lead busy, full lives. But despite its neutrality,

Switzerland had also suffered from the war and that was readily apparent.

At the beginning of her stay, Bette was rather aloof and avoided contact with her family. Then one evening after dinner as Bette was returning to her room, Greta came and knocked on her door.

"Am I bothering you?"

"No, of course not. I'm just very tired."

Greta paid no attention and sat down at the foot of the bed.

"Bette, my dear sister, I understand what you're going through. I've been through it myself, you remember?"

"Did you love your husband? I was madly in love with mine."

"I didn't love him madly, no, but I loved him."

"You see how different that is. Me, I could never make a new life with someone else."

"But you're twenty-two! You've got your whole life in front of you!"

"I could never do it."

"Bette, my angel, that's what you think today, you're still in shock, but you'll see life has a colossal force that will sweep you along without your being able to resist."

"Even if what you say is true, I could never abandon him."

"But Bette, he's dead."

Bette raised her eyes to look at her sister and contemplated confiding her secret, but she held back and breathed a deep sigh.

"Did you want to say something to me?"

"No—well, maybe, but I changed my mind."

"You can tell me anything."

"You wouldn't believe me."

"Go ahead, try me."

Bette told her sister about the apparition of Enguerrand and the anxiety she felt afterward. To her surprise, Greta showed no skepticism at all and nodded as though her sister were describing an experience she was accustomed to.

"Greta, did you hear me? You don't seem surprised."

"It's perfectly obvious that your husband wanted to say goodbye to you personally."

"Except he'd been dead for some minutes already and it happened sixty miles from our home."

"Have you heard of Rudolf Steiner?"

"Who's he?"

"A marvelous man—a philosopher, teacher, architect, and many other things besides. He started a center a few miles from here in Dornach. Tomorrow I'll take you there."

This was how Bette became acquainted with Rudolf Steiner and his wife Marie von Sivers, with whom she became friends.

The first thing that struck Bette upon entering the Goetheanum was its incredible overall atmosphere. The round forms of the center's architecture gave a certain soulfulness and autonomy to its structures, as though they didn't need the presence of man and were not even man-made. These buildings, designed by Steiner himself, became silent interlocutors—both enigmatic and imposing. The people who occupied them opened doors and closed them behind themselves without taking the least notice of the visitors. Then they would come out again quickly and go through another door, following some mysterious and invisible protocol.

"Who are these people?" asked Bette.

"People who are trying to rediscover the wisdom that we've lost over time."

"But what do they do?"

"Everything. Everyone works hard here. Steiner's teaching is infinitely rich in all areas. Anthroposophy is a path to knowledge accessible to everyone. Don't be intimidated. You'll see that everything will become clearer to your mind and to your heart."

"Is it a sort of university?"

"More or less. Come, we'll go to the woodworking shop."

A raised stage was set up in the middle of the workshop and several dancers were running here and there raising their arms and then closing them around an imaginary ball. Below the stage a voice was reciting some beautiful lines of German verse, but Bette was unable to identify the author. Bette was not yet the educated, ethereal, and slightly irritating woman she would later become. She looked around among all those gathered to see where the voice was coming from and finally noticed at the very end of the stage a strong-looking woman. Despite her hardy appearance and bold chin, she exuded an undeniably peaceful force as she read from a page with one hand and controlled the movements of the dancers with the other. She interrupted them several times and went onstage to demonstrate herself how the choreography should be followed. This was how Bette first encountered the bottomless soft blue gaze of Marie von Sivers, the wife of

Rudolf Steiner. Steiner himself then appeared through a side door and approached to watch the practice session. He was very attentive but never interrupted the proceedings. Bette allowed herself to be caressed by the warm, welcoming atmosphere, and by an antique beauty that was entirely genuine. She knew nothing about eurythmy, but was immediately drawn to want to know everything she could about it. Greta explained that it was not dance in the normal sense but more precisely an art intended to transform instinctive movement into conscious movement that would bring humans into a new harmony with nature and the cosmos. It was a kind of visible speaking.

"All that is pretty opaque to me, Greta. I don't really understand what's going on."

"Of course, my angel, that's perfectly normal. Explaining what eurythmy is to someone who has not tried it is like trying to explain what music is to someone who has never heard any."

When the practice was over, Steiner left the workshop and went to the amphitheater, where he was to give a lecture. Greta took her sister by the hand to present her to Marie von Sivers.

"Marie, this is my sister Bette, who has come from France."

"Hello, Bette, I'm very pleased to meet you. Everyone here likes your sister Greta very much."

"Well, the feeling is mutual, I believe."

The two women felt immediately at ease with each other, as though they were already friends. There was a deep and subtle bond between them from the start.

"What did you make of our little show? I hope we will soon be ready for our performance."

"Oh, Marie, I found you amazing as usual. Everyone was really great, I thought."

"You're too kind, Greta, but it's true that they are really inspired. But we can talk more later. Rudolf is about to begin his talk. Let's go listen together."

Steiner spoke vehemently about the culture's hostility toward the science of the spirit and he predicted a hardening of that hostility in the future. He claimed that studying the spirit was more necessary than ever to meet the changes going on in the world, but also that paradoxically this necessity aroused greater distrust and even animosity among men who were not inducted into that study. He said that the scientist of spirit or mind knew very well that certain devilish forces worked through men who were less evolved in order to bar the way to knowledge.

"What mankind needs the most will become the object of increasing attacks. The anthroposophy society is like a protective shield against aggression from the external world. But we who are familiar with these things, we must ask, from a scientific-spiritual standpoint, what are the most important qualities to instill in humanity. Two particular truths must be presented in a convincing manner: reincarnation and karma. What will be the implications for man when he recognizes that reincarnation and karma are true? Nothing less than the accomplishment of an amplification of the self beyond the predetermined confines of human knowledge acquired up until now. And beyond this enlargement of the confines of birth and death the feeling of responsibility is also amplified."

Steiner possessed undeniable charisma, and behind his round spectacles his dark eyes encircled with a bluish tint stared into your wounds, provoking at once both pain and relief. As hot tears were running down Bette's beautiful face, a weak light appeared in the depths of her dark thoughts. She reached out for Greta's hand and squeezed it.

"Welcome to your second family, my dear sister. You'll see it really is like a family."

"Oh Greta, everything is so overwhelming. I don't really understand what Mr. Steiner was explaining to us but I feel overcome with enormous emotion. It was as though he were speaking directly to my soul."

"That is exactly what he was speaking to."

"But what are these devilish things he was talking about?"

"According to Steiner, evil can operate in either of two ways: the way of Lucifer, which turns man exaggeratedly from reality, so that he only takes interest in spiritual matters; or the way of Ahriman, which binds him to matter and turns his attention from all spiritual activities."

"What would be an example? I apologize for asking all these naive questions but all this is so new to me."

"People who meditate all the time and neglect, for example, taking care of their children, would be dominated by Lucifer, whereas those who only think of money or power are under the total control of Ahriman. Is that clearer for you?"

In the following days, Greta and Bette would go off to the Goetheanum directly after breakfast. Marie von Sivers initiated Bette into eurythmy and even found she was rather gifted at it. They spent a lot of time together. Bette even told her the story of Enguerrand's mysterious appearance. Marie then told her a very similar story of something that happened to her husband at age seven.

"He was alone in the little train station where his father was stationmaster when a woman opened the door and walked toward him, making odd gestures as she approached. She told him that from now on he must do everything in his power to help her, and then she disappeared. Rudolf kept this a secret, thinking that sharing it would only provoke mockery and accusations of lying. Some days later, he discovered that at the precise moment he was having that experience a close relative had committed suicide. Rudolf was convinced that the deceased person had appeared to him to ask for help."

"So do you think Enguerrand came to me for the same reason — to ask for my help?"

"No, he would have told you. Come have lunch with Rudolf and me. I would be pleased to introduce you before he leaves again for Berlin."

The lunch was very lively and Marie von Sivers kept up a steady stream of praise for Bette's talented dancing. Bette felt loved and welcomed into this intelligent, warm family and said so.

"Well, you see you're not alone," Steiner replied softly. "Enguerrand will always be near you, but karma will bring other people into your life. Look to the light. His death was wished by higher powers, and things have ties that you must honor even if you don't understand them yet."

Bette's stay, which was to have lasted a few weeks, ended up lasting several months. She made friends with many people, including with a Russian eurythmist named Olga. The practice sessions were often very long. Marie von Sivers boldly declaimed texts in every language and remained devoted to the full artistic development of her students. She continually corrected, counseled, encouraged, and pushed them to better express their abilities. For their benefit she had given up on becoming a eurythmist herself, even though dance was her principal passion. Bette sensed the self-denial that led Marie von Sivers to confine herself to recitation and spoke about it with Olga.

"A few years ago," replied Olga, "she experimented with uniting eurythmy and recitation, and she had the two performed by the same person, but it was much less successful. To succeed, this totally new art needs to be carried by a highly artistic recitation, and to achieve that one needs someone who is capable of interpreting language anew in an agile manner. She is the only one capable of this high rendering that makes song and speech visible."

So that was more or less what eurythmy was about: making speech mobile and visible. Basically it made sense. If every form becomes speech, if every movement becomes speech, why not attempt the reverse? I had nothing against it except that Aunt Bette performed sample demonstrations for us many times and my brother and I found it all rather comical. But as I've said, we were just two snot-nosed kids scampering about far below the high sophistication of Aunt Bette.

Chapter Six

"Why did Aunt Bette return to France?"

It was almost dark out and I got up to turn on a light. Catherine had stayed listening to my story without interrupting once. I was rather surprised at her interest in my old family tales. With Luna it was different—she had to write a thesis, but Catherine's reaction surprised me. I have to say I was glad to have such an attentive audience; and what's more, telling my story allowed me to go back over events that certainly conditioned, without my knowing it, my family's whole existence, including therefore my own. The significance of this story about Bette went beyond the simple fact of her being an early avatar of a kind of new age worldview.

"I'll tell you about that, but it's getting late and I've not done anything about dinner. Why don't we go out and have seafood at the Procope, like in the good old days?"

By a stroke of luck there was a free table on the first floor. After ordering three plates of seafood and a side order of gray shrimp, Luna got up to go to the restroom. She came back smiling.

"I love those doors that say *Citoyens* for men and *Citoyennes* for women. This is such a great sanctuary of the French Revolution!"

"Every time I come here I think of my poor mother."

"She must not have liked the atmosphere."

"Certainly not! In fact, she never set foot here. When you think she used to call the Republic 'the beggar,' and at election time she would put toilet paper inside her envelope and drop it in the urn. The poor woman's existence was really a living hell."

At the next table a young man and woman were mooning at each other while constantly petting each other's hands. I glimpsed a look of longing admiration in the eyes of Catherine.

"I don't envy them in the least," I snapped.

"Well, Grandma, you're too old for that now."

"That must be it."

"No, I don't think your grandma was ever like that," Catherine said to her daughter.

"True, I was always too untrusting to abandon myself like that."

"But you must have missed out on strong emotions," my daughter added coldly.

"No, I never lacked big emotions, but I didn't seek them in that form of cannibalism."

"Are you trying to provoke me?"

"Of course not, Catherine, I'm just talking about the proper distance…"

"Schopenhauer's hedgehogs," interjected Luna to reduce the tension.

"Right. Mind the distance of the quills: too close, you get pricked too much; too far and you will lose touch."

"Nice couplet," said Luna laughing.

Catherine, my dear and only daughter, your sad face breaks my heart. Mockery is my only defense, don't hate me for it, my child.

What I like most about the trays of seafood is their smell that evokes the sea, the reefs with foamy waves breaking over them, the cry of gulls, and the fisherman's boat leaning to one side at low tide. The seafood plate is a marvelous window. Luna had closed her eyes an instant—I know she was inhaling the salty sea spray deep into her lungs. Catherine kept her eyes fixed on the black hole that was devouring her. How to get her out of that pit? I know there are words that heal, but I only know sarcasm and have no courage.

"Mom, are you all right?" asked Luna.

"No."

"Papa called you twenty times, you know. He ended up calling my cell phone because you never answer. He told me to tell you he loves you."

"And what did you reply?"

"That I didn't want to be in the middle and that those words ought not to be relayed by a messenger."

"Well put!" I said. "How does he expect to recover his wife by telling her through his daughter that he loves her? Really, I thought the Italians were sexier than that!"

That was my two cents and my preachy voice made even me uncomfortable. Luckily Luna, who has a better grip on her tongue than I, always comes to my rescue.

There are two possibilities: either my hippocampus has shrunk too much to filter my thinking, which I hear is common among the elderly; or else I am really an extremely timid person who cannot turn down being onstage. In either case, believe me, it's embarrassing and my pretty little granddaughter is not always there to generously pull my foot out of my mouth. She made some half-forced laughter, but her mother was so lost in her thoughts that she automatically smiled. I grabbed an oyster and heard the noise of a breaking wave and its retreat. This time I had an idea.

"Catherine, why don't we take Luna to Brittany? To your paternal grandparents'."

"But they're dead. The house belongs to Uncle Serge and you don't at all get along with Uncle Serge."

"True, and that's putting it mildly, but I thought we could show her the house from the outside and stay at a hotel. What do you think?"

"I think it's a great idea, Mom. I've never been to Brittany and it would help you take your mind off things," said Luna.

"Is it the seafood that's making you think of Brittany?"

"Why's that? Does Brittany smell like fish?" asked Luna.

So the next day all three of us were strapped into a rented Renault with our compass set in a westerly direction. During the five-hour journey Lorenzo called so many times that I lost my patience. It was impossible to complete a whole conversation or take a little nap without having Catherine's annoying ringtone go off in our ears.

"Okay, that's enough now! Either that phone goes out the window or you turn it off. Your Lorenzo is getting on my nerves!"

"But I like hearing his call and not answering. It's like when I was young and I'd hide when you were looking for me. I loved hearing you call 'Catherine, Catherine!' and as soon as you stopped looking and I was crouched like an idiot in my dark corner I was overcome with hopelessness."

"And did you leave your hiding place?"

"No, I stayed crouched and cried."

"Until I came, right? I did come, didn't I?"

"Always. And when you finally found me you were always exasperated!"

I understood perfectly what my daughter was describing, but I pretended to find her rather complicated, and so because I'm an old hypocrite I said, "You are certainly rather complicated!"

As a child, I kept up a total passion for my Papyrus and would have said or done anything to attract his attention — not hide from him. I therefore avoided telling them that on the way to church while Aunt Bette was holding my hand I dragged my heels enough to induce Papyrus to slacken his pace and come and pass his hand through my hair. But in fact Catherine was describing something else. She wanted to occupy me, occupy my whole head, my whole body, and all my energy. In fact this Lorenzo, I thought, might not be the only guilty party. He rang back over and over. I was so fed up I said nothing further and stared out the window.

We arrived at Saint-Briac around eight that evening, but in keeping with my flair for the dramatic, I insisted we go directly to the hotel without seeing the sea. A sea, and certainly the ocean, must not be bumped into casually. Preparations must be made, hopes built up. The ocean is…Christmas! More sublime than a forest or mountain. So one must get a first whiff of it, then search for it, then get a glimpse of its gray dress (because our shores are not blue or turquoise), and then finally walk before it with rapt attention. After depositing our suitcases in our rooms, we walked to a *crêperie* in the village center.

"Do you smell the iodine?" I asked my companions.

"No," replied Luna curtly.

"I only smell car exhaust," added Catherine.

"Oh, this is starting off well!"

"Grandma, it is starting off well, we just don't have your nose filled with scented memories."

"Catherine should have it."

"Well, I don't."

I kept my mouth shut again but I was rather bitter about the proximity of all this happiness that my troublesome daughter was determined to shove aside. Luna held my arm. I think she was taking pity on the old sentimental and tyrannical biddy that I might be turning into. Her gesture encouraged me to be generous. I pretended not to be offended and we were soon seated inside the cutest little *crêperie*.

"Luna," said Catherine, "you simply must order the Sarrazin crêpe with smoked salmon and for dessert you should order the crêpe with caramel and sea salt. If by chance you don't like those choices — though that's impossible — your grandma and I will finish them."

You might say that it doesn't take much to please me, and it's true that moment filled me with great joy. Catherine wanted to pass along these bits of memories. Particularly nice was the light, almost imperceptible joy that timidly animated her voice when she said "caramel and sea salt" and "impossible."

During our meal, Luna wanted to return to Papyrus and Rudolf Steiner.

"Don't forget you have to continue your story of Papyrus and Steiner. So far only Aunt Bette has become an anthroposophist."

"But Mom, you mustn't embroider too much," added Catherine of course.

"I don't embroider. Everything happened exactly as I'm telling it, my dear. If she likes this story, it's because it has real human feeling. In every story there's a human touch, and in mine there's me. I don't know how to be any clearer."

"I understand, but for example, Papyrus is described as a jolly, sunny force of nature who rolls on the ground with Uncle Gabriel, whereas I always heard him described as a depressive, self-destructive character."

"Yes, by my mother, or by people who didn't know him personally. Papyrus was the incarnation of joie de vivre, always fantastical and free. Certainly his way of life was not pleasing to everyone."

"Oh, come on, Mother, he abandoned you! And I know how he died!"

"Fine, my dear. Tell the story yourself then. You're getting on my nerves with your constant criticism. You know nothing about Papyrus. He died when you were only a baby. Papyrus was a marvelous person until everything tipped upside down."

"Everything tipped upside down?" It was of course Luna's young and innocent voice without the slightest prejudice, wanting to know more.

"Yes. It was always repeated that it was the war, but I don't know. He served in both world wars, obviously. He was a soldier. The Battle of the Marne had to have been indescribably awful. I can tell you all about that, if you like, but it happened long after his encounter with Rudolf Steiner."

Luna spoke to us about her life in Milan, her studies, and her recent love for a young lawyer. She told us all these things with disarming directness, without the least bit of girlie talk but instead a touch of self-mockery. Her large white teeth devoured with evident satisfaction everything her mother had recommended on the menu. She occasionally pushed rebellious locks of blond hair out of her face with the back of her hand. The charm of this child is poignant, like a flower growing at a dump. I believe I've never seen so much gracefulness, and immediately my heart was seized by the thought that she could be harmed. I don't understand how Catherine could be unhappy with such a treasure at her side.

The next morning we gathered in the dining room for a copious breakfast. The gentle early June sun was shining with all its might, warming the air filled with life and longings. We then took the car to the beach at the Grande Salinette. Luna seemed to find it a bit disappointing and I decided to show her what other marvels Brittany had in store. But this little beach was the one from her mother's childhood, and I wanted to go back there with her.

"Catherine, do you remember that kiddie club I tried to sign you up for?"

"Do I ever! It was torture! You know, Luna, for years your grandma pushed me to be a member of this kids' club and there was no way to make her understand that for me it was a nightmare."

"But you stared at it with such longing! I wanted to help you overcome your shyness. It was too sad. You absolutely refused to join and then you spent all your time watching them."

"Oh Mom, too cute! Were you really that timid?"

"Yes, terribly timid, and your grandmother wanted to force me to join but I was paralyzed with fear."

"It was for your own good," I said a bit too energetically.

Luna was walking with her head down and I thought to myself that I had made a mistake and that for Brittany to really have its full effect on her we should not have begun with the little beach of her mother's childhood.

So I said to her, "Don't think it's always so gentle around here. The Channel climate can be dark and stormy, you know."

We returned to the car to go see the seaside house of my husband's family. We parked near a picnic area and crossed the road to descend stairs that went down to the ocean. Old fishing boats seemed abandoned as well as some fancy boats. For hundreds of yards one could see them stranded on their sides, attached to buoys that comically served no purpose at low tide. The salty scents of algae were wonderfully exhilarating and I would have liked to run and run until I was out of breath, run barefoot across the sand to the other side of the bay, to another shore, to another time.

And I did, by watching Luna and her golden hair stirred by the strong wind of Brittany. She ran off laughing and with her arms spread out wide—behavior that looked to me like a gesture of gratitude for being so young, beautiful, and alive. Seagulls circled above our heads crying. Catherine walked with her head down. I wanted to tell her to look up, to stop concentrating on where she was stepping—she was so obsessed with falling—but I held off doing that and I was glad I did. She stopped and waited up for me.

"You see that rock there?" she asked me.

"Yes, that's where your father and grandfather jumped from at high tide."

"Exactly. I never knew how they could stand such cold water."

"Me neither."

"Shall we sit down there?"

"If you want to. I just hope I can climb up to it."

"Of course you can, you're ready for the Olympics!"

"The Olympics!" I repeated, gnashing my teeth a bit more than I would have liked.

With her help and a few bursts of laughter I managed to get myself on top of the rock. Then it was Catherine who laughed and it was enough to make me happy. She sat down next to me and we stayed there in silence looking out at our Luna, who had almost reached the other side of the bay.

"Hey, isn't that dangerous?" Catherine asked me. "She's not going to get trapped by the tide, is she?"

"For now don't worry. We'll just keep an eye on her."

"In silence."

"In silence."

"That's what you have the most trouble with, isn't it?" she asked smiling.

"That depends. When I'm with you, yes, you're probably right."

"With me? Are you kidding? I love silence."

"Maybe so, but me, I don't like silence with you."

"And why's that?"

"I always feel like you're reproaching me for something."

She stopped looking out where Luna was and turned to me with a look of surprise.

"That I'm reproaching you for something? What would I be reproaching you for?"

"I don't know, for giving birth to you, for example."

She turned her head back toward her daughter, who was waving her arms to tell us how happy she was.

"What a gift from heaven that child is!" I declared in sincere amazement.

That evening I decided to take them to Cancale to eat seafood. Catherine mocked me, predicting I'd come down with every food poisoning there was, including unclassified kinds. "All you eat is seafood now, and you eat tons of it!" I really tuned her out mostly, it had become like the ring of Lorenzo's phone calls — a tiresome white noise, but oh well. The evening turned out far better than our expectations: we had a delicious meal, lots to drink, a splendid view of the ocean, my daughter was in a better mood than usual, and Luna laughed at all my silly remarks.

On our way back, a full moon reflected its light on the water, where it made a broad stripe of a thousand shimmers. It was more than beautiful, it was proof that Catherine had nothing to reproach me for—all this grace belongs only to the living, she can thank me for being alive.

We stopped the car near the beach. The tide was high and Luna was sleeping in the backseat. Catherine and I walked hand in hand toward the sea, took off our sandals, and sat down near the water. She leaned her head on my shoulder.

"I have nothing against you, Mom. You irritate me sometimes, that's all."

"Oh, that's normal. You irritate me too, but I love you very very much."

"What irritates you about me?"

"Your discipline, your reserve."

"Do you think I'm mean-spirited?"

"What I think is that you don't take advantage enough of this marvelous gift I gave you."

"Well, me, what I find irritating about you is your egocentrism and petulance—it's really too much, you know."

"That should work in your favor though. I do everything. All you have to do is listen. I'd love to have a comedian around to do all the work!"

"But life doesn't have to be a series of euphoric one-liners."

"Well they help, believe me. At least they help me, and since you're like a wet blanket, never happy, always criticizing...Now hand over my bag, I'd like to smoke a cigarette and I don't want any back talk, okay?"

Suddenly the telephone rang and Lorenzo's face appeared on the screen.

"Oh, what a pain in the neck he is!" I spat out in exasperation.

Catherine turned off her phone and passed me my bag. To my surprise she took a cigarette out of my packet and lit it.

"You know that's really terrible for your health? With each puff the nicotine dilates your arteries and they become progressively less elastic until something horrible ends up happening to you..." I nattered on in my best Catherine imitation until I got a laugh out of her.

"Mom, I am so unhappy."

"Because of Lorenzo?"

"I am dying of jealousy."

"That is certainly no fun, I grant you."

"This is the umpteenth time he's cheated on me, you know."

"It's quite a good sign."

"Please! Stop trying to be funny and clever."

"But it's not funny at all! It hurts like hell! You're not the first or the last in that situation. The good sign is that he seems to have no intention of leaving you."

"Yeah, great, but all the while he's spending his time with these young bimbos!"

"It's nice to hear you get angry."

"I cannot continue like this. I have to find the courage to leave him."

"Are you sure of that? These are just passing fancies, don't you think?"

"Every time it chips another piece off the idea I had formed of our relationship."

"You have to admit that marriage is an enormously megalomaniac project when you think about it: loving someone for life, for richer, for poorer, in sickness and in health and all that. But fidelity, my girl, is a Mount Everest–sized ambition."

"But I've always been faithful!"

"Out of love?"

"Of course out of love! Not from pity!"

"Maybe from fear or out of laziness."

"Oh come on, did you cheat on Papa? Wait, don't answer that question!"

"Do you want my answer or not?"

"No, no. I don't want to know."

"Fine."

"Oh my God, so you did!"

"Listen, Catherine, if you want me to tell you, I'll tell you, but get a grip on what you want, would you?"

"Okay, so don't tell me anything."

"Cheating is merely the desire to go ashore on an island, even a tiny island, even a not very pretty one. As soon as the ship has dropped anchor, it begins to dream of the ocean. Cheating is just a little curiosity mixed with a dose of narcissism. Most ships go out to sea again after the little pause on shore."

"And where's love in all that?"

"Love is the ship. The captain does not abandon the ship at any port of call."

"Yes, but I have the right to kick him off."

"What's certain is that if it makes you that unhappy, he should stop doing it. On the other hand, you should not spend your life rehashing this stuff. It's banal, it's human, and it doesn't mean he's stopped loving you. He'll never leave you, but you, you need to ask yourself if you're going to continue to live like this or if you're going to take off for good, because there is life beyond Lorenzo and his daily planner and his absences and his incessant phone calls."

"Sometimes I get the feeling you're defending cheating."

"No, I'm defending the right to make mistakes, that's all. Life is, along with its tortuous beauty, very complicated."

With her thumb and index finger, she flicked her cigarette butt far into the water like a seasoned professional. Catherine was perhaps not as naive as she seemed.

Chapter Seven

From Wikipedia:

THE BATTLE OF THE SOMME (French: *Bataille de la Somme*, German: *Schlacht an der Somme*), also known as the SOMME OFFENSIVE, was a battle of the First World War fought by the armies of the British and French empires against the German Empire. It took place between 1 July and 18 November 1916 on both sides of the upper reaches of the River Somme in France. The battle was intended to hasten a victory for the Allies and was the largest battle of the First World War on the Western Front. More than 3 million men fought in this battle and one million men were wounded or killed, making it one of the bloodiest battles in human history.

The French and British had committed themselves to an offensive on the Somme during Allied discussions at Chantilly, Oise, in December 1915. The Allies agreed upon a strategy of combined offensives against the Central Powers in 1916, by the French, Russian, British and Italian armies, with the Somme offensive as the Franco-British contribution. Initial plans called for the French army to undertake the main part of the Somme offensive, supported on the northern flank by the Fourth Army of the British Expeditionary Force (BEF). When the Imperial German Army began the Battle of Verdun on the Meuse on 21 February 1916, French commanders diverted many of the divisions intended for the Somme and the "supporting" attack by the British became the principal effort.

The first day on the Somme (1 July) saw a serious defeat for the German Second Army, which was forced out of its first position by the French Sixth Army, from Foucaucourt-en-Santerre south of the Somme to Maricourt on the north bank and by the Fourth Army from Maricourt to the vicinity of the Albert–Bapaume road. The first day on the Somme was, in terms of casualties, also the worst day in the history of the British army, which suffered 57,470 casualties. These occurred mainly on the front between the Albert–Bapaume road and Gommecourt, where the attack was defeated and few British troops reached the German front line. The British troops on the Somme comprised a mixture of the remains of the pre-war regular army; the Territorial Force; and Kitchener's Army, a force of volunteer recruits including many Pals' Battalions, recruited from the same places and occupations.

The battle is notable for the importance of air power and the first use of the tank. At the end of the battle, British and French forces had penetrated 10 km (6 mi) into German-occupied territory, taking more ground than in any of their offensives since the Battle of the Marne in 1914. The Anglo-French armies failed to capture Péronne and halted 5 km (3 mi) from Bapaume, where the German armies maintained their positions over the winter. British attacks in the Ancre valley resumed in January 1917 and forced the Germans into local withdrawals to reserve lines in February, before the scheduled retirement to the *Siegfriedstellung* (Hindenburg Line) began in March. Debate continues over the necessity, significance and effect of the battle. David Frum opined that a century later, "'the Somme' remains the most harrowing place-name" in the history of the British Commonwealth.

Chapter Eight

Papyrus and his cousin Vincent were both twenty-one when they left for the front. Geoffroy was two years older. I know nothing about what happened then, if they returned home often, or how they found the strength to withstand the horror. I imagine it changed them a lot, that war was so bloody and they were so young. All I know is that they were fighting close to our home in the department of the Somme and that Papyrus for some unknown sentimental reason had placed the medal of the Virgin Mary around his neck. My mother regularly told us the story of the medal, it was her war story, the victory of faith over the battlefields: a German bullet lodged in the center of the medal without Papyrus receiving the least scratch. He may have been a rowdy fellow, but that experience appears to have shaken him into thinking he'd better marry the young, timid girl who had given him the medal. He must have considered her like a guardian angel, and since she was his neighbor and not unattractive, he decided to be patient and ask her to marry him.

According to my mother, at the moment Papyrus caught the bullet with the holy medal, the Germans were launching an offensive in the area near her family's little château. She used to say, and each time with the same emotion, that her father ran to the village church to join the priest and eat all the sacrament wafers before they fell into enemy hands.

"Wouldn't it have been better to fight to keep the Krauts from taking them?" Gabriel asked one day.

"But can you imagine what it would have meant for our Savior Jesus Christ to have fallen into the hands of those butchers?"

"Why? Because the Krauts don't believe in Jesus?"

"You don't understand, Gabriel, that your grandfather was a hero, and Abbé Delvaux too. They held communion for hours without a thought for the debris that was falling down around them, the pieces of woodwork and the crumbling walls. They carried out this communion slowly, praying with each host for the salvation of their souls and the souls of the French. I would be very proud of you if one day you had to do the same."

"Okay, but I think that Papyrus was a real hero, he fought and so did Uncle Geoffroy and Cousin Vincent... and all the soldiers in the trenches too."

"Of course, but your grandfather was an even bigger hero because he was serving God first of all and France came just after."

Gabriel didn't want to hurt our mother's feelings, but her story, which we'd heard since we were very young, lost its prestige little by little as we got older. As children we thought our grandfather was admirable, and if our mother had not constantly gone back over it, we would have kept a heroic impression of him. The problem was she didn't have many other stories in her repertoire. There were only about one hundred people in our village. There were a few château owners in the area that we were more or less related to, but she wasn't a gossip or mean. In fact I think she was fairly ignorant. I never saw a book in her hands other than the biography of some saint or other. She spent her days occupied by the morning mass, managing the domestic servants, meals, five o'clock tea, and a few social calls where she was either the hostess or a guest. At six o'clock she went to her room to repeat prayers. Then she prepared dinner and voilà! — another day was done and another step closer to eternity had been taken. What a horrible life! But let's go back to before her marriage to the end of the First World War.

Papyrus resumed his military life between adventures, balls, and mistresses of every kind. The only woman that he, Geoffroy, and Vincent thoroughly respected without question was Bette. While she was back in Basel at the home of her parents, those three companions spent lots of their leave time in Paris at the home of Vincent's mother, our rich and worldly aunt Gertrude, who had fled as best she could their sad country home in Picardy. It was there that Bette reappeared in 1920.

Papyrus and his companions would sometimes smoke opium at the home of the Count de Redan, an old partier who organized sumptuous, refined soirées. He liked inviting these three musketeers, whom he found amusing and available. Debauchery united them and they often spent the afternoon in one of those red salons decorated with Asian fabrics and motifs. They would recline on comfortable mattresses while an old Chinaman prepared the opium. Papyrus claimed that they also carried on serious philosophical discussions, but I don't know how much that is to be believed.

Spiritism was very fashionable at the time and the salons of the nobility were filled with mediums and stories of the dead communicating with the living. Papyrus participated in all that without taking it seriously but simply to go along for the ride with his friends, who found it intriguing. During one alcohol-soaked evening at the home of Charles de Redan, Papyrus was introduced to a stunning young woman from America, Julia Stenton, who claimed she communicated with the spirit of Kate Fox, the youngest of the three sisters who had launched the vogue for Spiritism in the United States and then in Europe. The Fox sisters lived in Hydesville, New York. After regularly hearing knocking coming from inside the walls of their house, the women imagined that it could be the dead trying to communicate. They developed a kind of code in which a given number of knocks corresponded to a letter of the alphabet. It was in this way that a certain Charles Haynes became known to them and claimed to have been assassinated in the house before the Fox family moved there. The three sisters pleaded with their parents for a search to be undertaken, and that search led to the discovery of the remains of a human skeleton. This story created an enormous sensation and the Fox sisters toured the country retelling it. The young women attracted the attention of scientists as well as the curiosity of the general public. When it was revealed that they were using some gimmick during public attempts to communicate with the beyond, the Fox sisters' prestige rapidly declined, but the passion for Spiritism persisted and made its way around the globe.

After dessert, guests were invited to return to the drawing room, and Julia Stenton asked for complete silence. She and six others sat at a round table. They each placed their hands down on the table with outstretched fingers lightly touching. Papyrus and Charles de Redan looked on from a few steps away.

"Even Doctor Ribaud is indulging in this game. I can't believe my eyes!" exclaimed the Count.

"Indeed, now we've seen everything. You should perhaps change doctors, unless, that is, you don't mind having your prescriptions written out by ghosts."

"Yes, and look at your aunt Gertrude and that air of the possessed."

"True, but with her it's different. She follows every fashionable turn in the road. If tomorrow's high society were to begin exercising on balance beams, Aunt Gertrude would become a gold-medal gymnast."

Julia Stenton was unable to enter into contact with Kate Fox and had to make do with Victor Hugo. The Count's guests were impressed to hear the table make loud noises to answer yes or no to questions or to indicate letters of the alphabet. Papyrus became bored and said his goodbyes. He returned along the river and was happy to be by himself. He walked with a lively step as usual, though he had no particular amusement in mind, nor did he feel sleepy. He noted the long gray silhouette and shadow of the Eiffel Tower. He thought of Guy de Maupassant, who apparently often liked to dine there because it was the only place in Paris where it could not be seen. At the Pont Royal he stopped to contemplate the Seine and the moonlight reflected in the water. He was tempted to let himself feel sad, but chased the idea from his mind and resumed his walk back to Aunt Gertrude's residence.

The following week, Papyrus, Geoffroy, and Vincent were again in the Count's home smoking opium. A heavy-set gentleman with a mustache spoke out in short breaths to describe a newfangled body language, the materialization of music, and an art of movement that was being called eurythmy. He was telling everyone of his keen interest in these new forms of expression that aspired to an ideal and in the spiritual mission of the artists who practiced them.

"Is this another one of those Spiritism exercises that my friends and I love so much?" asked the Count with a dry mock.

"Not at all! Nothing to do with that! You have to see it to believe it. The vogue for Spiritism is ridiculous; anthroposophy on the other hand is a true science of the mind. One mustn't confuse them! I have a good Swiss friend, an anthroposophist, her name is Elisabeth de Louvenel, and she will be giving a performance of eurythmy to some friends this evening. Come along with me if you like."

"What's her name did you say?"

"Elisabeth de Louvenel."

"My, what a coincidence! She's the widow of our old friend Enguerrand de Louvenel! Of course we'll come along and give her a little surprise while we're at it."

Having never taken drugs myself, it's not easy for me to describe exactly the mind-set of these three men who were forever united by Picardy, their childhood, and the untold horrors of war. What I do know is that on that evening they were in sufficiently good form to knock at the door of the large residence near Trocadéro that belonged to the Count and Countess von Sonnenreich, two charming Austrians who welcomed them warmly. Once inside they were able to set about organizing their surprise for Aunt Bette. Their hosts served them champagne in lovely Baccarat crystal glasses as well as the most exquisite petits fours. A string quartet was playing Schubert in a corner of the drawing room and in the next room one could see a stage had been erected at one end. The elegant yet cozy atmosphere and the joy of seeing Bette again must have been strong enough for Papyrus to overcome the visceral displeasure he felt upon hearing German spoken, or perhaps that came later with the Second World War. In front of the stage three rows of chairs and a sofa had been arranged to accommodate about thirty people. The Countess gracefully came forward and turned to the audience with her back to the stage.

"This evening, our friends Elisabeth de Louvenel, Anette Morgenstjerna, and Olga Berdiaeva will interpret an extract from Goethe's *Faust*, the 'Walpurgis Night.' You all know the importance that Rudolf Steiner gives to this piece from *Faust* within his admirable understanding of the spiritual world. Our friends will be performing for you this remarkable example of eurythmy, which we owe to the immensely talented Marie von Sivers. I will now let the movement speak for itself."

The Countess then gathered her long green satin dress and sat down in the middle of the sofa. The three dancers arrived onstage with light, lively steps. They were dressed in white outfits adorned with colorful veils. Bette wore a pink veil and the other two dancers wore yellow and orange. They ran from one end of the stage to the other before coming to a halt in front of their public. They then each held one arm over their hearts and with the other seemed to be grasping something out of the air. A man's voice emerged from among the onlookers and recited a text in German that the three friends didn't understand in the least, but since they were probably still high on opium, they found the whole thing very pleasant. The three women continued their odd but elegant and expressive choreography. Bette, totally absorbed in her art, didn't even notice them. At the end of the performance, which was enthusiastically applauded, Bette disappeared to change into a proper dress embroidered with little gray beads. She wore a matching diadem in her hair and she was all the more striking now that a period of mourning had removed an excess of healthy pink naïveté. Her eyes were wilder, her voice deeper, and her steps more catlike. She showed every sign of being enchanted to see her old friends.

"What a wonderful surprise! I can't believe my eyes! I never would have imagined finding you in a situation such as this! From now on we shall be inseparable! I want to learn all about you, every minute of everything you've been doing in the past twelve months. And how is Picardy doing? And my in-laws? I abandoned everyone to pursue this marvelous adventure of anthroposophy. Oh, we have so much to tell each other! Let's never separate ever again!"

The three musketeers were immensely flattered by this warm reception, even though they didn't understand much of what Bette was telling them.

"Bette, my dear," Geoffroy finally dared to say, "what is all this you're talking about? We are only soldiers and don't understand a thing about all this anthroposophy business."

"There will be plenty of time for me to tell you all about it, but what did you think of the performance? Did you like it?"

"Oh very much," they all replied warmly.

They spent the rest of the evening evoking pleasant memories of Enguerrand and their friends. Bette also asked for news of her new sister-in-law. Papyrus didn't hesitate to share the strange story of how she saved his life with the medal and Bette was enormously stirred up by it—so stirred up in fact that they found it worrisome. Then with a pale and distant stare she pronounced these oracular words:

"So many signs mark the way. It's up to us to open our eyes and notice them. Do you understand Louis,"—Papyrus's real name was Louis—"that my sister-in-law protected you from a distance with the force of her love?"

"I don't believe in that sort of thing, you know, but all the same I was very struck by it, no pun intended."

"Where is the medal?"

"I always carry it with me. It's in the pocket of the coat I left in the vestibule."

"Would you mind getting it? I'd like to see it."

Papyrus was only gone a minute and then returned with the medal and handed it to Bette. An elegant Russian gentleman joined their little group and Bette introduced him.

The Russian took the medal in his hand and reacted enthusiastically to the miraculous story.

"It's indeed quite amazing, I agree," said Papyrus. "But I don't believe in the supernatural one bit."

"And so what do you make of it? Purely an accident?" asked the Russian in impeccable French.

"Naturally. I must seem rather rough around the edges to you, however…"

"However, you keep it in your pocket," Bette interjected softly.

"Yes, because it was given to me by a pure and innocent hand, and after all, this little piece of silver did save my life."

"It's really quite amazing," repeated the Russian, taking the medal in his large hand again. "You know, I too was until recently quite skeptical of such things, but lately I've been coming upon more and more bizarre incidents."

"For example?"

"Do you know my good friend, the painter Wassily Kandinsky?"

"No, you are probably the first Russian I have ever met."

"Well, Kandinsky is in my opinion the greatest painter alive today, but that is not why I bring him up. The reason is he told me about an experience dating back a few years that left him rather upset. After a lively dinner with his friends Thomas and Olga von Hartmann, they decided to try to talk with ghosts by turning a plate with an arrow and the alphabet around the outside. They were then stupefied by the contact made with a female spirit named Musutsky who had lived in Ufa in Bashkiria, where she is buried. She asked them to pray for her cousin and she spelled the first three letters of his name: *S, H, A*."

"Yes, but your Kandinsky and his friends may have been having a collective hallucination."

"That is precisely why he wrote to the priest in Ufa to ask if he had known a parishioner by that name."

"And what was his reply?"

"He replied one month later that the cemetery contained many named Musutsky, but only one with a cousin named Shatov. Rather curious, don't you think?"

"No, most likely just a coincidence. You will not convince me."

"But that is not my aim," said the Russian laughing freely. "I'm not sure I'm convinced myself. I simply wonder at it, that's all. I'm humble, more humble than you are."

"So you only believe in physical matter, Louis, despite what this little medal tells you?" said Bette.

"I believe in God, but I maintain a strict boundary between the world of the living and the dead."

"There are so many things that we must talk about, my dear Louis," whispered Bette as she took him by the arm.

The four met again frequently and ran into each other at the same social events. I know that Vincent soon became tired of Bette's theories and started going to Paris less often. He had also begun courting a young, levelheaded Norman woman whose lighthearted teasing turned Bette's earnest theories into uproarious laughter. That woman would become our aunt Elodie.

Chapter Nine

On our way back to Paris we stopped off at the château of my maternal grandparents. Luna wanted to see where my mother was raised. We began at the cemetery—that seemed like the normal thing to do. My mother and her parents as well as Enguerrand and Aunt Bette were all buried there. I felt a little guilty about not having gone back there for many years, but really she was the one who chose to return to her origins instead of being buried somewhere more accessible for her children. My poor mother—everything she did irritated me. I did the introductions and Catherine crossed herself. Luna and I did the same, feeling a little self-conscious about not having thought of it on our own. I did, however, say some nice things to my mother in a low voice, and I greeted my grandfather, the communion wafer muncher.

We next went on to the castle. We first stood in front of the iron gate and contemplated it. Of course for Luna and Catherine it must have looked spectacular, but I immediately spotted broken shutters, unruly grass, a broken-limbed eucalyptus lying scattered in the garden. One should not retrace one's steps, one quickly smells death and abandonment. All the same it was not unpleasant to be alive in the company of these two women I love and who give meaning to everything I lived through.

Luna took a few pictures and Catherine asked me some questions about where the bedrooms were and the layout of the other rooms. Luna was rather proud that her family could claim to have such a glorious estate in its history—we all laughed. She then asked that we go see Warvillers, where I had grown up, but I was not too pleased at the suggestion. I didn't dare say that to her and we were very close by.

"You won't see anything, you know. It's well hidden by a forest of poplars and an allée of plane trees."

"But we'll ring the bell. Just like in the movies, we'll ring and say that the daughter of the Count of Corbois wishes to see her old bedroom."

"And they'll answer, 'The daughter of the Count of Corbois does not live here and if you want to see her look her up in the phone book.' No one remembers us, and it's a good thing too, given the scandal back then. I assure you I'm quite happy that they've entirely forgotten us!"

"Come on, let's at least try!"

She took out her smartphone and entered the address in Warvillers. It was a fifteen-minute drive away. How could I disappoint her and say that what for her was just another story was for me like returning to a house filled with vampires? I got back in the car stoically and let the proposal go forward. My mother's castle was already having an effect on me. After all, it was the place where Aunt Bette had lived out the end of her life and Gabriel and I had spent a lot of time in our younger years. But the house of my childhood was another matter entirely.

Luna, however, was filled with interest for these bits and pieces of my past life. We parked in front of the gate. My legs felt like jelly. Unexpectedly, it was Catherine who came to my rescue: "Luna, it's not really a good idea, you know."

"No?"

"No."

Luna glanced at me in the rearview mirror. I looked at her and said nothing.

"Of course, I'm sorry, it's just that you're such a good storyteller I felt like I was in a movie."

We got back on the road to Paris. The sky was gray.

I was careful not to point out that Catherine's phone had been silent all day. When we reached the highway the sky was black and I wondered if there was going to be enough time for us to get home before the heavens let loose.

We rushed to park the car near Place Saint-Sulpice and ran to my entryway just as the first heavy drops of rain were coming down. What a relief to be together, and dry, in my building. I was thrilled at the prospect of having a nice little dinner with a nice bottle of Burgundy while the storm raged outside, and I sensed that my girls were also savoring the moment. Then when I turned to unlock the inside door we all saw a letter on the doormat. It was addressed to Catherine—just *Catherine*, with no other writing or stamp. The fellow must have come and left it himself.

"But how did he get inside?"

"He must have got the concierge to let him in, or a neighbor."

"Oh great, Mom, so anyone can just come into your building whenever they like! You should really do something about that."

"Settle down, my dear. We'll hire a bouncer if you like, but for now would you please just open the letter?"

"It's from Lorenzo."

"Yes, well, I'd guessed that."

She opened the envelope delicately and I stood thinking how very different we were. Luna and I stood there nosily trying to interpret her facial expression as she read. I held the keys in my hand and a far-off ambulance broke the silence.

"He's here. He's at the Relais Saint-Sulpice in the rue Garancière. He wants me to go meet him there."

Catherine kept looking at the piece of paper—a cruel doubt gripped her, it was clear. I wanted to tell her that her life was not at stake, that a couple's duet does not turn on one note, that what brings on its downfall is never-ending, complicated, and brimming with good intentions.

She is so afraid of making a mistake that she forgets to ask if she still loves this man who showers her with presents but sleeps with women who are younger, slimmer, and funnier. Does she really know what she wants? Does she want to be desired or cheated on and indemnified? Catherine has lost track of herself within this long and banal marriage saga.

She stared at the key hanging in my hand as though she expected it to give the answer. I opened the door and the three of us walked in. The thunderstorm was going full blast. I turned on all the lights, but despite the golden, welcoming light of my living room a nervous feeling came over us.

"Okay, I'm putting on some makeup and going."

"Oh, wait at least for the rain to let up a bit, you'll get soaked."

She didn't listen to me, and after three minutes in the bathroom she rushed off, telling us she'd keep us informed.

I couldn't help peeking out the window as she crossed Place Saint-Sulpice, hunched over and holding her umbrella like a shield. She seemed nervous and powerless and that broke my heart.

Luna offered to prepare some pasta for us and we went into the kitchen to pull together a meal. I was startled by each clap of thunder. My idea of the three of us huddling together in my cozy living room was shattered. Instead I became extremely anxious thinking of my daughter crossing the square amid thunder and lightning to go off to that man who didn't love her as much as she'd like. I had never been an apprehensive mother, and look at me now in my advanced age and how I felt lacerated with worry. Or maybe I was always more afraid than I ever allowed myself to admit. When she used to hide and I'd call her like an idiot and get no response, I remember how severe but contained my irritation was. In fact I always had the impression that I was putting her in danger by having her in my care. I knew full well that I was not up to the task—too nervous despite my courageous air, and too responsible not to have understood the mad act I had committed. And so why then did I have her? It couldn't have been from love, since we didn't know each other. When she was young,

Catherine would put her little feet into my shoes and she'd walk around the apartment as though she were on a cross-country skiing expedition. She looked funny and I wondered what pleasure her awkward movements could be giving her. Maybe that was why I'd had her, so that she'd step into my shoes after me, after I wouldn't be going anywhere anymore. And then love got in there and as always complicated everything, simplified everything, or let's say explained everything. My greatest love story is her. And now suddenly I'm petrified at the idea that a bolt of lightning might strike her. Since that moment when she leaned her head against my shoulder in Brittany I've become the mother of a child again.

Luna and I ate in the kitchen. Her pasta was delicious and she was talking on gaily but I didn't have the heart to join in. I could only think of her mother.

"Do you think we should send her a text message to ask if she got to the hotel okay?"

"But Mamie, the hotel is just behind the church, right? She's there for sure! You can see the square is empty. I didn't know you were such a worrywart."

"A worrywart? No, certainly not, but really this is quite a storm we're having this evening."

"That's for sure. I just hope he's at the hotel."

"Oh my God, and what if he went out?"

"But Mamie, she's got a brain, she'll call him in that case! Don't worry. If he came all this way to bring her back, they're not going to get lost wandering around Place Saint-Sulpice!"

After having some herb tea in the living room, we both went off to bed. Luna was tired of course, she had done all the driving. The storm had subsided and in its place came a strange silence. In darkness behind the window I looked out at the square, which was oddly empty. The night is so beautiful when one has it all to oneself.

Chapter Ten

I often wondered how Aunt Bette managed to convince Papyrus to accompany her to Munich to listen to Rudolf Steiner give a lecture. Uncle Geoffroy I could understand, given what happened later, but my father—it was really an odd occurrence. Nevertheless, in 1922 Papyrus, who hated the Germans, didn't speak German, and who had no elective affinity for spiritual matters, found himself attending the last lecture that Rudolf Steiner would give in Germany.

At the time Steiner had just published *The Renewal of the Social Organism*, which became a best seller. That book set out his ideal society, which he based on a "threefold social order" analogous to the order of the human body and onto which he also grafted the ideals of the French Revolution: liberty, equality, fraternity. Briefly stated, he affirmed the head as the sphere of culture and creativity. To it must be guaranteed the liberty that every individual needs for self-realization. The senses and the circulatory system correspond to the realm of politics and the law, and every person must be guaranteed the same rights. Finally, the economy corresponds to the metabolic system, and the priority there is fraternity or solidarity. Riches are to be produced for the collectivity and not merely for individual profit.

These ideas, though considered utopian by most politicians, who hardly paid any attention to them, were pleasing to many people during the chaotic postwar era. They also brought down on him a good number of enemies. Marxists were hostile to the influence he had within the working class, which he was supposedly diverting from the true revolutionary combat, while the far right detested him for his antiwar declarations and his call for the abolition of borders. In short, Steiner's life was not simple. I say all this without the least pretension of being an expert on the topic, I'm only passing on what I can still dredge up from my spotty memory.

As soon as they arrived in Munich, Papyrus realized he was not fond of this city, which seemed to give off an aura of uncertainty. It's important to underline that Bavaria in 1922 was a bit topsy-turvy. The dissolution of the monarchy was still fairly recent, the prime minister Kurt Eisner had been assassinated three years earlier, and one year later in 1923 there would be Hitler's putsch and the imprisonment of the future führer. The social climate was unusual to say the least. For Aunt Bette things were different. She was Swiss, loved modern art, and she would have followed her passion for anthroposophy to the ends of the earth. She therefore ran off to every new exhibition, while Geoffroy and Papyrus discovered the city and its churches with the aid of a thick guidebook. Bette had given them instructions to meet her at the Frauenplatz for lunch. She arrived with rosy cheeks and a big grin on her face. She told them she had seen the most wonderful paintings, so filled with spirituality and freedom that she couldn't get over it. The two men listened to her patiently, but were probably thinking more about what they were going to order.

"I recommend the *Schweinsbraten* with potatoes, and after we'll have *Apfelstrudel*—how's that sound?"

"Perfect," replied Geoffroy politely, while Papyrus, who was resigned to everything, looked out the window at the large brick church that dominated the square.

"Is that their cathedral?"

"Yes," said Aunt Bette, "it's the Frauenkirche, like our Notre-Dame. Go inside, it's worth it."

"Someone spoke to us about a very nice lake a few miles from here, I'd like to go there if it's possible."

"Steiner's lecture is the day after tomorrow and we return to France the next day."

"Okay," said Geoffroy, "then we could leave for the lake this evening and stay there until we come back for the lecture. What do you think?"

"You will not have seen very much of Munich."

"Yes, but for me," Geoffroy insisted, "I'd really like to spend some hours on that lake."

Aunt Bette cast a puzzled look at Papyrus, who was careful not to oppose his brother. She therefore yielded, though perhaps a bit disappointed by this change in their program.

"Okay, I'll see about renting a car that we can take to Lake Berg tomorrow morning, and I'll reserve three rooms for us."

The two brothers were very relieved to see that the unpronounceable things they'd ordered off the menu turned out to be a delicious pork roast and an excellent apple tart with raisins. They drank beer with their meal and after rounding things off with a little plum schnapps were feeling quite jolly. Aunt Bette then took her leave to continue the errands and visits she had lined up, insisting that she didn't have much time left to do everything she wanted to accomplish. The brothers called to the waiter to settle the bill and then went off to visit the cathedral.

"Say, Geoffroy," asked Papyrus, "what made you want to change Bette's program?"

"I hate this place."

"You hate it? Really?"

"Do you like it here?"

"No, but I don't mind staying two more days."

"Not me."

Uncle Geoffroy was calmer and less unsettled than Papyrus, but when he got something into his head he could be as stubborn as a mule. They entered the cathedral, which they both found remarkable.

"I prefer ours in Amiens."

"*Oh là là*, Geoffroy! Are you turning into an anti-urban hillbilly?"

"That's right, I'm a chauvinistic provincial. So are you, you just don't want to admit it. This is the first time either of us has been out of France, don't forget."

"So it's normal to feel a little out of sorts abroad."

"If we were in Rome, I assure you we wouldn't be feeling the same way," Geoffroy snapped back.

"I admit it's a bit odd to find ourselves in Germany after all those bastards did to us!"

75

During this whole exchange, they advanced toward the Gothic nave. Suddenly something hit the stone floor at their feet with a light metallic ring. Since there was not much light, they had to bend over to search for the unknown object. Papyrus then discovered it was his holy medal, now resting in the middle of a footprint with a little tail near the heel.

"Oh my, it's the medal that saved my life!"

"What's it doing there?"

"I have no idea!"

"It must have fallen from your pocket."

"Yes, it must have. I'd been looking for it for a while and couldn't find it. I must have forgotten that I'd put it in this pocket."

"Show it to me. It's still got the bullet lodged in the middle. That is really unbelievable."

"Yes, unbelievable. And to think I never thanked that child."

"That child must be a beautiful young woman by now. Brother, it's time to go thank her!"

The two left the church and went strolling through the streets, smiling at the lederhosen that they had never seen before. They bought themselves two long ivory pipes that had deer-hunting scenes sculpted on them as well as two fancy hats topped with pheasant feathers. For Bette they bought a delicate coral cameo.

In the evening, after having freshened up, shaved, and changed clothes, they met Bette in the hotel's large drawing room. She looked splendid in her emerald dress, which matched her big green eyes, and they both made the same movement to take her arm. She smiled, took one arm on each side, and they strode into the dining room where a chamber orchestra was playing Strauss. From the beginning of their stay Geoffroy had tried to take the lead. He ordered champagne and other items off the menu as best he could understand them. Bette looked on amused. She then announced that all was ready for their departure the next morning to Berg on the shores of Lake Starnberg.

"You'll see it's a very nostalgia-filled location, but since you're determined, we'll go there."

"Lakes are always nostalgia-filled," replied Geoffroy. "It's their prerogative. Do you know why?"

"Because they're always dreaming of being as big as the sea and yet always confined by their banks," said Papyrus.

"It's because their water is troubled and their strong winds cannot transport it anywhere except to the opposite shore," added Bette.

"Or perhaps it's because they enclose their shoreline inhabitants in a vicious circle. It's a closed universe that does not regenerate and dies its own slow death. Nothing new enters and nothing exits, everything is continuously recycled, that's what makes the lake atmosphere so heavy," Papyrus concluded.

"So tomorrow we'll sleep in the village where King Ludwig II of Bavaria was found drowned in very mysterious circumstances."

"Why do you say that the people along the lake are more shut in than others?" asked Geoffroy.

"I've observed it," said Papyrus.

"But what are you saying? Geneva is full of foreigners!" Bette shot back.

"Perhaps," said Papyrus. "But it's clear that coastal people are more open to otherness."

"Picardy residents, for example, are very welcoming. They're so open they even marry Swiss women!" said Geoffroy with a knowing glance at Bette.

"Oh my goodness," Bette sighed, "I certainly feel guilty toward our Picardy relations. Since the death of Enguerrand I've not gone back there, I receive news only rarely, and myself I only write at holiday time. But what do you expect? He was my reason for being in Picardy. And you, do you receive news from Picardy?"

"It's curious that you bring up the Louvenel family. If you can believe it, just today while we were visiting the cathedral, the medal that your young sister-in-law gave me and that I thought I'd lost fell from my pocket."

"Oh, and so you suddenly found it again?"

"Yes, by a stroke of luck, because we were in the nave and it was quite dark. It had fallen into a recessed footprint set within a yellowish stone."

"The *Teufelstritt*," Bette murmured as her face whitened.

"The what?"

"The *Teufelstritt*…It means the devil's footstep."

"Okay, here we go, now what's that all about?" asked Papyrus half in jest and half irritated. "Really Bette, you spend too much time with these anthroposophy sophists!"

"Say what you like, but it's rather odd, don't you think? This medal that saved your life disappears and then reappears at the very place where according to legend the devil was standing when he mocked the 'church with no windows' designed by the architect Halsbach. And it's true that from that precise spot if one is looking at the altar, one cannot see any windows."

"So our marvelous Bette believes in the devil."

"Your Ahrimanian spirit keeps you from evolving, Geoffroy. You are drowning in the material, completely deaf to the language of spirit. I pity you."

"No Bette, don't be offended. You know us, we're just simple, unsophisticated cavalrymen."

"Yes, but I don't like your teasing."

She was very beautiful pouting like an angry young child. Papyrus enjoyed being with her despite her odd notions. They were total opposites. She was ethereal, communing with the stars, while he was stuck in the mud of his war memories. She soared high among the eternal wisps of spirit while Papyrus and Geoffroy remained grounded in the reality of the trenches. If they followed her to Munich, it was certainly not out of devotion to Rudolf Steiner and certainly not on account of her charming almond eyes. They followed her because she was a ray of light that penetrated the black sticky wall of their nightmares. The only price to pay was putting up with all these odd conversations.

"I would even say, my dear Louis, that you should not waste another minute and go ask my young sister-in-law to marry you. She must be of age to get married now, and it would seem to me that all signs clearly point in that direction."

The next morning, a hired car brought them to Berg on the shores of Lake Starnberg. The weather was lovely and as soon as they'd deposited their bags at the hotel they went out for a long walk. The climate was pleasantly cool. The sun and the little waves lapping the shore harmonized tranquilly with the surrounding forest of beech trees. Bette ran ahead crying to them, "I'll hide. You try to find me!"

To give her time to find a hiding place, the men walked away from the forest and closer to the shore. Across the lake they could see the Possenhofen castle, where the Empress Sissi was raised. They let a few minutes go by and then split up to try to find Bette. It was then that what was bound to happen happened.

Papyrus walked off to the right toward the hotel, while Geoffroy went left toward the little chapel erected at the place where Ludwig II of Bavaria is said to have died. It was Geoffroy who found her crouched behind some ivy bushes, and when Papyrus finally turned and came back he found Bette and Geoffroy in each other's arms lost in a passionate kiss. It's true Papyrus was not the stuffy type, but it must have shaken him up a bit to find himself suddenly the odd man out within their little trio. He turned quietly and walked back to the hotel. Later that evening when they all met up again, Bette and Geoffroy acted as though nothing had happened.

Back in Munich they barely managed to arrive on time for the all-important Steiner lecture. Bette was as giddy as a teenager at her first ball. As for the men, they dragged their heels plenty, but they had promised and promises mattered even to these rough-edged rakes. The Four Seasons Hotel was packed and they had to squeeze their way through the many attendees. The lecture was entitled "Anthroposophy and the Knowledge of Spirit" — just reading it elicited yawns from the two cavalrymen. Bette's fanatical zeal gave her the courage to fight her way to the front row. Rudolf Steiner arrived onstage, his pince-nez dangling from a little cord.

"I really want to introduce you to him at the end of the lecture. You don't speak the language, but it doesn't matter. Let yourself be transported by the sheer energy pouring out of this man. Don't try to understand him, just let yourselves be gently rocked. Can you promise me that?"

Aunt Bette would not be able to introduce anyone, because as Steiner was attempting to lay out his thinking with a charisma that even the two roughnecks had to acknowledge, a certain brouhaha broke out and disturbed the proceedings. A man hurled an epithet that Bette translated for Geoffroy and Papyrus.

"Oh dear, they're calling him a traitor. They're nationalists and they've sworn to get rid of him!"

Everything happened very quickly. Steiner's supporters, who luckily were more numerous than the small group of nationalists who had come to assassinate him, surrounded the speaker to protect him. Bette, Geoffroy, and Papyrus were among those who gathered around and brought him to a side door that allowed the unhappy lecturer to get away. Everything happened so quickly; afterward Bette was visibly shaken and in tears.

They escorted her back to the hotel and all the while she said the most incomprehensible things.

"They'll kill him, you'll see. Those men are servants of Ahriman, they will destroy him."

The two men tried to calm her, but Bette was all stirred up.

"All these signs we've been sent: the medal falling on the *Teufelstritt*, the Russian friend who tells me worrisome things. I know you're here to support me and that you don't understand what I'm telling you, but you saw with your own eyes what happened, didn't you?"

Papyrus left the two of them. He found himself back at the Four Seasons Hotel without realizing it. This city was not without its charms, but he and Geoffroy both felt similarly disoriented there. Bette's crazy notions could not persuade a man like him, and yet an inexplicable low-level anxiety had come over him. He felt as though Munich were in the grip of hostile subterranean forces. Occult forces? Certainly not. Ahriman was not the jailor of Munich, but there were, without a doubt, postwar troubles and an unsettled political climate in this country that had so recently emerged from monarchy. How was he to explain to Bette that there was nothing more dangerous than man in his abominable material being, and that there was nothing spiritual about it—of that he was one hundred percent certain.

So that was how Papyrus met Steiner. But I should add that Steiner's influence on later events would continue, through the offices of Aunt Bette, naturally. As I retell all this I realize how much of it is at the origin of many later events that would mark our lives. I had never really thought about it before, I was so preoccupied by holding together the thousand different pieces of our existence. As for Geoffroy and Bette, they became so serious that on the way back to Amiens, Geoffroy proposed and she accepted.

Upon his return, Papyrus went to knock at the door of his future father-in-law to see what had become of little Marguerite.

Chapter Eleven

I saw a documentary on television about something called music therapy, I think. This technique is being used to treat certain cases of dementia, autism, anorexia, and similar disorders. But what I found most striking was the use being made of it with children who have motor skill problems. A little boy in the film who had great difficulty walking had chosen to focus on the violin. Whenever he moved, even a little bit, the sound of a violin was instantly triggered. In this way he was taught that his movement had an impact on the environment. It's important to realize, explained the therapist, that when we move from point A to point B we are affecting the world around us, even if we may not notice it.

For the young patient the violin that accompanied his movements testified to his ability to change the order of things. If we were really conscious of how much each of our actions affects the rest of the world, we might not dare to do anything. If Aunt Bette had not discovered Steiner, perhaps she never would have saved my life.

Catherine did not return to the apartment until lunch-time. She was very pale and her makeup had run. She gave us one of those tired smiles that signals an all-out fight and a Pyrrhic victory that comes too late after too much effort.

She gave a loud kiss to Luna and caressed my cheek.

"Are you all right?" I asked timidly. "Do you want to eat some of this nice mâche salad that Madame Joseph prepared for us? Here's some cheese and a nice fresh baguette."

"Great. I'll get myself a plate and utensils."

She left and came back to sit with us. We were very curious to know how things had gone but pretended we weren't so as not to overwhelm her. Especially me — obviously the overeager mother is immediately suspect. Thankfully Luna couldn't stand the suspense and as soon as her mother had sat down, she launched in.

"So?"

"Luna, don't leap at your mother, let her tell us what she wants to."

If one's going to pretend, one might as well go all the way, even though I risked killing the momentum started by my granddaughter.

"My dear, what can I say? He asked me to forgive him. We talked for a long time. He begged me to return to the house. That's it."

"And so things are exactly where they were before," said Luna, clearly annoyed.

"In a way, yes. Oh, Mom, he wants to speak with you. He's very intent on explaining something to you."

"Explaining what? That it's difficult to remain eternally in love even when one deeply loves someone? That's very nice, but tell him I'm already very familiar with the whole business."

"You hold it against him?" Catherine asked.

"Not against him as a man, but as a son-in-law."

"But you're not going to give him the silent treatment?"

"Of course not, what do you think!"

After lunch Catherine went to lie down and I stayed with Luna. Lorenzo had gone back to Milan. Luna told me about her boyfriend.

"In September he's going to Toronto for six months to study because he got a scholarship, then he'll return to Milan. I'd like to go with him."

"Well, do it then!"

"Mom will hit the roof!"

"Oh no she won't, I won't permit it. She'll miss you, of course."

"She's not like you."

"Oh no? Are you so sure? When she went off to live in Italy I wasn't too happy, I can tell you that. But what can you do? That's the way it is with children. You spend your life either wanting them to be happy without you or disappointed when that's exactly what happens. It's the most ambivalent and complicated of relations, and the whole thing is inevitably sprinkled with bad faith since what mother will admit to being a cannibal? For fathers it's different. The uterus creates special complications, don't you think?"

"Mamie, I've not had kids, so I have no idea."

"For daughters too it's complicated. My mother, for example, I hated her so much and loved her so much too. I felt constantly betrayed by the differences between us and she probably did too. As though the fact of being of the same flesh created in one and the other the expectation of being absolutely identical. When really everything set us apart."

I felt slightly dizzy and when I tried to stand I passed out.

When I came to, noise of a commotion all around made me anxious. A man leaned over me and said, "Madame, Madame, do you hear me?"

I stared up at him in surprise. What was he doing in my home? I looked at the others around him. One was kneeling at my side taking my blood pressure. I looked about for something familiar and saw the silhouette of Catherine standing behind them. She had a serious look on her face.

For Pete's sake, Catherine, what's going on? And what are all these people doing here? And why am I lying on the ground?

"You're going to be taken to the hospital for some tests, Madame. Don't you worry, everything's going to be fine."

I'll worry if I want to, for heaven's sake! Catherine, don't let them take me away. Who are these people with all these tools? What do they want with me? Come my daughter, you're not going to leave me in the hands of these strangers, are you?

She stood there like a statue and did nothing to defend me. I had no choice but to surrender.

She looks sad though, scared even. That's probably why she's not reacting. She's scared stiff. Catherine my dear, get a grip on yourself and stop these people from taking me away. I'm too tired to resist, but you, you can do it. But the stretcher is already going down the stairs and I'm on it. All I need now is to have them drop me. Damn it Catherine, do something!

They are kind and considerate, and yet in no time there I am lying down inside an ambulance that's moving through the city with all its sirens blaring.

I was afraid like I've always been afraid — in silence and perfectly immobile. Fear always paralyzes me, and it's better like that, it shows less that way.

At the emergency room, a kind nurse caressed my hand before sticking a needle into it with a plastic tube attached, all the while talking to me as if I were a baby.

"It's going to feel 'ouch,' but you're going to be a big girl and cooperate nicely, okay?"

As for being a big girl, yes I was a big girl. The cutie-pie nurse had no fear of euphemisms, that was for sure. As for cooperating, I really had no choice, so stick me with your needle, my pretty, and drop the obsequious patter. And this is what she did in fact, and with a little smirk of joy that didn't escape my notice.

"Bravo, you didn't budge. You are truly a model patient."

I'm not a model anything, I'm terrified and I'm certainly not going to pick a fight with a nurse holding a needle. She's got to save my life! It will take whatever it takes. As for Catherine, thanks for sticking up for me...not! She's totally missing in action. Probably off crying in some corner instead of organizing my liberation. Papyrus, if you were still here, I would have nothing to fear, but stay where you are and don't expect me to join you right away. I still have some matters to resolve first.

Next came a string of doctors, some of whom were rather condescending. And then an endless series of tests. Blood tests, urine tests, heart tests, and on and on. I was taken aback by all this interest. Really, all this devotion to human life even when the life in question was that of an old relic like me. My place was in a museum, if there is a museum for the old and ordinary. Instead of that, I found myself in a famous hospital surrounded by competent healthcare professionals, all with such good intentions. And yet I would have given anything to be at home, and the worst thing I could imagine was dying amid all these good people. In the hospital my death would be really clear and final, whereas at home it would be enveloped in a big sleep, and I preferred that.

Ah fear! Fear is so invasive. It's impossible to see clearly and to reason. And without the ability to reason, vertigo entirely takes over.

Christiane is a little devil but she is very intelligent. My mother used to say that, but since I considered her to be rather stupid I never paid her any mind. Christiane is devilishly lively and what's more very intelligent, my father would say, but since he was my father, I only half believed him.

When Papyrus took me in his arms, I would fall into a frenzy of laughter—a great but precarious happiness. He preferred Gabriel and it was always Gabriel who got tossed into the air. I also believe it's this bit of abandonment and isolation that made me intelligent. Gabriel was too happy to think—at least in our earliest years. Later things changed for him too.

I was born in 1929. Papyrus and my mother had been married for five years, and I think he was already feeling bored with her. In any case he was so happy to have a daughter that he sacrificed his most handsome oak tree to build a baptismal font. Abbé Chaivreaux officiated at my baptism. Cousin Vincent was chosen as my godfather and Aunt Bette as my godmother. She was Protestant but this was not really a problem except for my mother, who held back her tears and accepted the arrangement despite reservations.

Poor Mother! She could never stand Bette and had to put up with her twice over as sister-in-law!

The first years of my life were very cheerful times. Papyrus had a talent for inventing games and lively parties. Between masquerade balls and hunting, picnics, blindman's buff, and hide-and-seek, our childhood was awfully privileged and happy. I say awfully because the high price to be paid eventually came due. Gabriel and I were spoiled and rather poorly raised, I believe. With our playful father and weak mother, we became two wild, insolent little brats.

Uncle Geoffroy and Aunt Bette lived in the château at Rochebrune a few miles from Warvillers. I don't remember exactly the reason for this, but I think it didn't bother my mother, who preferred to have the château remain in the family. Since after the death of her parents my mother and Bette were the sole inheritors and since Bette had received a generous inheritance from Enguerrand, it was normal that she take up residence there. Furthermore, being rich, she could afford to make many improvements to the château, and it quickly became far more luxurious than ours.

I know no one is listening to me, but I'm telling my story because it's the only thing I can focus my mind on. It's said that old people have a very weak memory of distant things but that recent events are kept solidly in mind. Perhaps. Me, I think we have an insatiable need for certainties, and that when the present appears more fleeting than ever and the future is hidden under a threatening opaque veil, there is not much besides the past that one can count on for proof of one's existence.

I was born in 1929. I am eighty-six years old and I have the story of Papyrus to tell.

But there's no stopping their constant interruptions, bothering me with a thousand little tortures that I'm yielding to without the slightest protest since I'm obliged to go along with the unshakable faith in life. Here's the pretty nurse who thinks I'm stupid coming back.

"So, since you were so kind and cooperative, you get a prize."

I knew I had every reason to avoid making any fuss.

She left and came back with a disgusting food tray containing drunkard's vomit, a little frog diarrhea, and bile jelly. She could dream on if she thought I was going to eat that. What would I have received if I'd been uncooperative! She must have taken pity on me since she said: "Well, look at the face you're making! Come on, time to start eating on your own like a grown-up. I'll go fetch your surprise."

Ouf, so that wasn't it. She came back with Catherine and had the grace to leave us alone together.

"Mother, how are you doing?" She rushed over to kiss me.

"I'm just a little tired, but please, please get me out of here quick."

"You will leave as soon as you're able, Mom. But first tests have to be done to understand what happened to you."

"Oh, good God, after all their exploring, I assure you if there were anything to know they would have found it by now."

"We have to wait for the results, Mom. Please, just let them do their job and do what you're told for once."

"Ach, this obsession with infantilizing the infirm! Just because we need help does not make us stupid!"

"I get that you're furious, Mom, but look, that's the way it is. So show a little patience and quit the capricious whining."

Fine, Catherine, fine. I know you're right, fine. But I'm going to stay silent to punish you all the same.

"But the food, yuck, what a disaster."

"Ah, so you agree with me?" I spat out triumphantly. "How could anyone eat that garbage? It reminds me of a Mark Twain story where people are forced to eat eggs with baby birds inside as a way to cure them of their pickiness."

"I think I'd rather eat a bird raw than that disgusting gruel!"

"Couldn't you at least find me a piece of baguette and some Camembert?"

"And maybe a half-bottle of Burgundy while I'm at it, right?"

"I'm not kidding, Catherine, they're going to kill me with this crap."

"So skip a meal! It's not going to kill you, so stop worrying!"

The nurse returned to see how I was doing and made a series of patronizing remarks.

"This is not good, Madame. I give you a surprise and you're being naughty. Am I going to have to punish you and ask the woman to leave? Is that what you want?"

I shook my head vigorously to say no, and Catherine came closer and caressed my forehead.

"I don't mean to tell you how to do your job, but she doesn't have much of an appetite, you know. I think she must be a little shaken up by all that's happened."

"She doesn't have to eat it all, just a little. Come on, a few spoonfuls and I'll leave you alone."

I shot Catherine a look of pure terror. She was evidently looking for a way out of this situation but was also afraid of challenging the authority of the nurse. It is so difficult to be dependent on others.

"No, please, don't force her. She'll eat tomorrow, I promise. Leave her alone tonight, she's had a really tough day, you know."

Mercifully, the nurse backed off, but still kept up her obsequious smile. Peaceful resistance had worked. I felt like jumping for joy.

Catherine stayed with me to the end of visiting hours and left as it was getting dark.

We spoke a little about her meeting with Lorenzo, but I quickly understood that her suffering was actually linked to her feeling of resignation. She was not ready to forgive because she already feared the next round of suffering, and yet she was unable to break the tie that was causing her to suffer so much. It was a kind of Stockholm syndrome, but where the jailor was not Lorenzo but instead the first years of their relationship, when everything was simple and corresponded to her romantic imagination of things. Later ugliness emerged — in the folds of routine and under the mask of complicity there was hidden the grimacing face of boredom. She had satisfied him from cellar to attic with a thousand little inoffensive habits, but he felt a nostalgic urge for wide-open spaces and sought out a compromise in the beds of young adventurers. His love was hers but the feeling of wind in the hair came with young strangers.

The doctors returned and promised to transport me to a room the next day.

Anxiety came over me. I was alone, a captive in this sordid room with the pretty nurse whose solicitous air made me panic.

I was born in 1929 and Papyrus would organize the most extraordinary treasure hunts.

Chapter Twelve

We were well into the month of July when Papyrus organized the most beautiful of all his treasure hunts.

He had divided us into two teams. Gabriel was the captain of the first team, which included François, Benoît, and Henrietta, the cook's daughter. Pascal, whom I was secretly in love with, was the captain of my team, and there was also Gilles and Isabelle, who was very pretty and very well behaved, and this made a big impression on me.

Like every year, Papyrus gathered us together in the living room and then distributed identical envelopes to the two captains. In each was the first clue. The goal was to find the hiding spot of the second envelope without the other team following your trail. Pascal grabbed the envelope from Papyrus's hands and we scampered off as fast as we could to hide from the inquiring glances of Gabriel and his teammates, who did exactly the same thing for the very same reasons. Isabelle was a born leader and I would have given anything to be like her. But her hair was straight, shiny, and dark, while mine was frizzy and blond. She was considered careful and discreet, while I was fidgety and nervous. She was sweet and serene, whereas I was always at war against something or someone. I had tried to straighten my hair to look more like her, and when I was alone in my room I would practice speaking like her and imitating her delicate hand gestures. The result was my hairdo took hours to complete and only lasted a few minutes. As soon as I started running behind some dog or after Gabriel, *bam!* my disorderly curls would bounce back as before. As for my imitations, the day Gabriel surprised me while I was rehearsing I was so upset that I never dared do it again.

Anyway, there we were trying to solve the first riddle. It was a rebus that directed us to Father Ledoux's barn. We all arrived screaming, and the moment the two captains reached out their hands for the second envelope, the delicate, charming Isabelle reached out and snatched it. Because it was her, no one said anything, but had it been anyone else it would have provoked a real brawl. The game continued with a series of riddles, rebuses, and other puzzles. I never guessed any of them and it bothered me that I appeared like such a ninny. When a solution seemed silly to me, I gave up, even though it always turned out to be the right answer. Clearly a setback on my way to becoming a leader. But with all those boys, me being a little assertive was unthinkable.

What I remember perfectly is the last part of the hunt, which ended up in the large clearing behind the Rovachole farm. This time our team had a big advantage, because the others hadn't understood a thing about the riddle. Unfortunately, we couldn't race across an open field and through the forest to the farm quietly. Gabriel and his teammates, not understanding the riddle, decided to follow us. We were a little ahead, but the race was an all-out breathless affair. We were the first ones to get to the clearing, where a spectacular surprise awaited us: a hot-air balloon! It was an enormous balloon with red and yellow stripes. Papyrus was aboard looking magnificent with his leather helmet and goggles. Gabriel took advantage of our shocked surprise to leap onto the wicker basket and get himself hauled inside. Papyrus pulled him in by his britches. I was steaming mad. I rushed toward the basket too. Once inside, I went after Gabriel and pummeled him as hard as I could. Papyrus was laughing but nevertheless separated us.

"It's not fair! We guessed the last riddle! Why did he get to climb in first? We figured everything out first, Papyrus. All they did was cheat and follow us." As soon as I felt his hold releasing me I went after my brother again and gave him a good kick.

"Christiane, that's enough now. If you don't stop you won't be coming with us!"

"Well, I won't go then. I'm not going up in the sky with cheaters!"

"Okay, then get down and let the others climb aboard."

If Papyrus had known how much he had broken my heart at that moment, he would never have said such a thing. As for Gabriel, when I think about it today I still feel like wringing his neck.

They all climbed into the basket one after another while I walked away sobbing. A little while later, however, after I'd been kicking at the grass and thinking of the worst imaginable punishments that could be visited on them, and especially on my brother, I heard Papyrus call me. I turned around to see him running after me saying, "Christiane, Christiane, come back!" But instead of throwing myself in his arms I ran off faster to escape him. He eventually caught up with me, I probably wasn't even six years old. I resisted him with all my strength, but he only laughed at my efforts.

"Christiane, my little wild thing, we're waiting for you to take off. We're not leaving without you. You don't want to keep your friends from having this beautiful trip into the clouds, do you?"

"I'm not going if my stupid brother Gabriel is going."

"But we're all going!"

"Then what was the point of solving the riddles if everyone gets to go?"

"Come on. Stop being so stubborn and get into the balloon."

He took me in his arms and hugged and kissed me. He laughed while gently teasing me. I think in my whole life I never felt a love as full, compact, and total. Papyrus, I loved you so much.

Papyrus taught us how to ride a horse. My brother was a talented rider and totally fearless. I was terrified but I couldn't stand the idea of being left out, so I would grit my teeth and pretend to be enthusiastic. Mother didn't take care of us much. I have few memories of her that don't have to do with prayers, polite behavior with visiting aunts, and the occasional scolding that was no doubt well deserved. It was important to her that at least in public we be more or less presentable. She had drilled us fairly well in basic manners, but it was important that the show be as brief as possible because our ability to play model children was very limited.

Our lives rolled on sweetly and without incident. Our mother probably suffered, but we were not conscious of it. Papyrus continued to go back and forth between his military base and the château, which seemed sad without his lively presence.

We attended the village school and were all together in the same classroom. Madame Gilbert did her best to attend to the level of each pupil. I was really good at French and history, but had rather disastrous results in all other subjects. Thankfully she would test us in a low voice while the others were doing their assignments. Isabelle, who had long, impeccable braids with not a single hair out of place, always held herself so straight in her pretty pale pink apron. She answered questions in perfect cadences with her hands clasped behind her back. I would have liked to do the same, but except with grammar and poetry, I was incapable of any cadence, since I remained as mute as a fish. Of course my mother made some negative remarks at report card time, but since Papyrus expressed total indifference, I concluded that I was taking after him with my mediocre school performance. Gabriel's results were not so great either, but he was really good at math. Sometimes we bartered homework between our strong and weak subjects, but when I had to explain what I was doing we always ended up in stupid arguments. And yet as soon as we separated we would become totally bored. At bottom Gabriel and I were completely united — in hate and in love.

One time when he was on leave, Papyrus came home with a motorcycle and sidecar instead of a car. You can imagine our excitement. He took us for a spin—me on the back hugging him around the waist and Gabriel in the sidecar. Back at the château we stubbornly refused to get off and made him ride around a second time, but with me in the sidecar and Gabriel behind Papyrus. Gabriel had less fun that time because it's true the sidecar is really something special! The experience gave me one of my first life lessons: those who begin by doing what they prefer so as not to die before having got to it don't really know how to manage their pleasure. In my view it's crucial always to go in the direction of improvement. But really, life is a screwed-up hodgepodge and one can't know for sure how to improve it.

For my mother the motorcycle and sidecar was a terrible experience.

Papyrus made her get on behind him and took off at full speed toward the forest, where he had fun taking sharp turns—so much fun in fact that once back at the château he didn't notice that Mother was nowhere to be seen. He left his motorcycle in the garage and went off to drink tea quietly beside the fire.

Geoffroy and Aunt Bette stopped by and the three of them fell into cheerful conversation. Some time went by before Papyrus took them out to see his new toy.

"Wow, fantastic! And does it go fast?" asked Geoffroy enthusiastically.

"Very fast. A while ago I was really having fun in the forest. Want to take a ride?" Suddenly he turned as white as a sheet. "Shit, shit, shit!" he said.

"What's the matter? What's gotten into you?"

"Marguerite! I lost Marguerite!"

He then jumped on his vehicle and sped off toward the forest, leaving his two guests in puzzled amazement.

He found Mother in tears at the base of a beech tree, in pain everywhere and deathly cold. I don't know if she was suffering more from her wounds or from having been so ignominiously forgotten. He picked her up in his arms, placed her in the sidecar, and then returned home at a gentle speed. I think he was horribly embarrassed.

Mother did not talk to him for weeks after that, even though he seemed finally more considerate. I remember being very surprised at his kindness toward her, and maybe that was in fact why she hesitated to make peace with him. She must have been terribly afraid of losing what little respect her sprained ankle, fever, and bruises had won for her.

When it came to our misdeeds, the solidarity between me and Gabriel was total. But one day he did something for me that was truly generous, even though for once he was unquestionably innocent and under no obligation.

Papyrus's Bavarian pipe had a place of honor on a little table between two red velvet-covered armchairs positioned near the hearth. When he would come back from a walk or get up from a meal, he would always sit in the same place, fill his pipe, and smoke it with manifest satisfaction. His silver tobacco case engraved with the family's coat of arms was always full and I loved the smell of it. One day when I was feeling lonely and bored — Gabriel had been kept after school and Mother was as usual hiding in her sitting room doing embroidery—I took the pipe and a pinch of tobacco and went off to steal some matches from the kitchen. I went up to my room and imitated all of Papyrus's gestures: I filled the pipe, lit it, and sucked on it while twisting my face as he would do and letting air pass to the side like a giant fish. The smoke burned my throat horribly and I started coughing uncontrollably. Young and inexpert, I had even forgotten to open the window to get rid of the smell. It was around six p.m. and Arlette, our attractive maid, entered to get the bed ready for the night.

"Christiane, what is all this smoke?" she exclaimed, rushing to open the window.

I seized the moment of her back being turned to stash the pipe under the bed, but the noise I heard there made me more nervous still.

"Have you been smoking? Christiane, where's this smell coming from?"

"I don't know. It must be from outside."

"No it's not, and in fact it's less strong now that I've opened the window. And what about these matches? What are you up to, Christiane?"

"Nothing. I just wanted to burn some papers."

"And where are they, these burnt papers?"

"Listen, Arlette. I will never do it again, now leave me alone. Nothing bad has happened, okay?"

"Okay, but you give me back those matches right now, and if I catch you with them again, I will repeat everything to Madame the Countess."

"No, please don't! I'll be spanked and sent off to say prayers!"

"Ah, you are truly insolent, but you do make me laugh!"

Arlette really loved us and we loved her. She was very young and attractive with her rosy cheeks. She had a very welcoming bosom and when we were young Gabriel and I used to love resting in her warm embrace. Now we were a little too old to be granted such favors. Given to laughter, refreshingly cheerful, and tender—Arlette was the complete opposite of our mother. However, at that moment I just wanted her to scram. Since she had all the beds to prepare and the dining room, she didn't stay long. She simply shut the curtains, folded down my bedspread, placed a pitcher and water glass on the bedside table, and passed the bed warmer between the sheets.

As soon as she closed the door behind her, I rushed to look under the bed with beating heart, almost fainting, and discovered what I had been fearing all along: Papyrus's pipe lay broken into three pieces. I was dizzy from a rapid-fire series of thoughts and emotions. What should I do? Commit suicide? Perhaps. But maybe I should see if there wasn't another way out. Should I get rid of the pieces? He was likely to lecture all the servants and it was also likely that, to avoid injustice, Arlette would say what she'd come across in my room. Should I accuse someone? I had my faults but I was not up to doing that. Especially over a crime that I had committed myself. I was desperate. In fact the only option was suicide—while hoping to be unsuccessful, of course.

At that moment Gabriel burst into my room and threw his school bag on the ground.

"What a jerk that Benoît is! Because of him I had to stay after school."

I was petrified by my predicament and couldn't speak.

"What's wrong with you? What a face you're making!"

I remained speechless, tears in my eyes. Images of my long fall into shameful desolation continued to pass before my eyes in slow motion. I was emotionally and physically exhausted.

"Hey, what's the matter? Have you seen a ghost or what?"

In a way, yes, I had imagined the ghost of my "failed suicide" with me lying in a real pool of my own blood. Better that than unleashing the wrath of Papyrus.

"Hey, are you going to tell me what this is all about or not?"

I held out my dirty hands holding the broken pieces of pipe and burst into tears. He took them, now with his own lugubrious air.

"Oh shit, how did you do that?"

I told him the whole story as best I could, but I was crying so much that I had to start over from the beginning several times. He listened to me, serious and silent. I sat on the bed and he sat next to me and put an arm around my neck.

"Do you want me to say I did it?" he asked in a knotted-up voice.

"No, you'd get such a beating! I'll have to confess, but I'm really afraid."

"Listen, we'll say it was me."

"But aren't you afraid?"

"Of course I am, but less than you, I think."

"He won't let you go in the sidecar anymore."

"For a long time do you think?"

"I don't know. Neither of us ever did anything this bad before."

"Well, too bad, we'll still say it was me."

"No, I can't accept that."

"How shall we tell him, and when? As soon as he gets back? Or should we write a letter?"

"But the letter will arrive after he's already back."

"Should we tell him as soon as he arrives or wait until he notices the pipe's missing?"

"No, as soon as he arrives."

"That way there'll be no dessert, but too bad."

"I'll save you my whole piece and give it to you later."

During the few days that remained until Papyrus's return we were so mortified that we behaved like angels. At the end of each meal that we ate with religious solemnity I offered my portion of rice pudding or crème brûlée to Gabriel, but his stomach was as knotted as mine.

The following Saturday, when we heard in the distance Papyrus's motorcycle approaching, I said to Gabriel, "Listen, I was the one who did this dumb thing, so I'm the one who should be punished."

"You didn't see your face the other day! You don't have the nerve. We're saying it was me and that's final."

"That makes me feel awful, Gabriel. I don't want you to miss out on the sidecar."

Papyrus was already at the front door.

"So, my children, you don't come and kiss your father anymore? No sidecar today?"

We went up to him and put out our hands.

"Look at you both! What's the matter?"

Gabriel, trembling slightly, showed Papyrus the pieces of pipe.

"I'm sorry Papyrus," he said in the smallest voice.

"What happened? Did you knock it over?"

Gabriel nodded without daring to say a word.

"That's a pity. I'd bought it in Monaco with Geoffroy. I'll try to glue the pieces together and keep it as a souvenir at least. Get in the sidecar and we'll go see if we can find a similar one in the village."

He bought a less beautiful pipe that day but it allowed him to have a smoke in his customary way.

When Papyrus died and Gabriel and I were dividing up his few remaining possessions, we came across the repaired broken pipe. I insisted that he keep it. Having been so loyal and courageous, he deserved to have it. After that pipe drama, I became more patient and generous with my brother—my jealousy was dissolved by my infinite gratitude.

Chapter Thirteen

The next day I was taken to the cardiology wing. I shared a room with a young woman who looked about forty. She had a sweet air and a beautiful smile, which made me like her immediately. She told me to call her Josephine. She had fainted while leaving an Odéon movie theater and that's how she ended up in the same hospital as me.

"Just like that with no warning?"

"I hadn't eaten anything plus I'd been really hot. When I stood up I didn't feel well but I did manage to leave the cinema and then, bam, lights out!"

"Just like me! I hope you liked the movie at least."

"Nope, it stunk actually!"

"Since my husband's death I don't go to movies, even though I live only a few doors from where you were."

"Oh really, where?"

"Do you know the church Saint-Sulpice?"

"Yes, of course. Everyone knows Saint-Sulpice."

"It's the only church I know besides Notre-Dame. Churches aren't my thing."

"Me neither, I'm Jewish."

"You're Jewish?"

"Does that surprise you?"

"No, but I never would have guessed."

"Because I'm black, perhaps?"

"Yes, that must be it."

"You're not the first person to find that surprising!"

I was amused by how sincerely puzzled she looked. Our lunches came. This time the odor was worse than the appearance. I must have made such a pitiful face, for she bounded down to the foot of her bed and seized a brownish pasty substance that was on my tray.

"So you find it disgusting? Me too."

She took whatever it was immediately to the toilet and flushed it away along with her own portion. She then returned to her bed after placing the empty container on my tray.

"Mission accomplished. A yogurt is not going to be enough for you, but I have some apples and cookies. We'll get by with that."

"My daughter will be here soon and we'll ask her to go buy us something. We can do that, right?"

"Just avoid asking."

She rinsed an apple and handed it to me. By the early afternoon my daughter had still not arrived, but Josephine was completely engrossing and I was extremely curious to learn her life story. Her mother, a French teacher and a Jew, had married an atheist poet from Cameroon. She had spent her childhood in Cameroon and moved to France about twenty years ago. She worked at a little bookshop in the rue Caulaincourt. She earned a meager salary but her love of books made up for it somewhat. She also got along with the landlord and his family.

"And do you have a family? A husband I mean, and children?"

She exhaled slowly with puffed-out cheeks and turned toward the window as if to find in the clouds some refuge from my prying questions.

"I'm sorry if that was nosy of me. It's sort of the way I am, you see."

"You're not being nosy, it's just that I still have scars, you understand."

"Better than you know. You can imagine that at my age a person has accumulated a goodly number of wounds and scars."

"And are you married?"

"I'm a widow and I find it painful. He took everything with him. Everything that I was before becoming an old lady. In fact, it's since he died that I've really become old."

"You're in mourning for him and for yourself?"

"That's exactly it."

"Je suis envahi de brume / Et de solitude / Aujourd'hui, / Et je fuis."

["I'm invaded by fog / and solitude / today / and I'm fleeing."]

"Who's that from?"

"Léopold Sédar Senghor, the great Senegalese poet, do you know him?"

"No, I only know of him, but I like those lines."

"Really? That pleases me. My father venerated him and recited his poetry often."

I liked Josephine a lot.

Catherine arrived around four p.m. She looked annoyed on my behalf to see that I'd been assigned a double room with someone else, but I told her how pleasant my roommate was and that calmed her down. Luna also arrived with a box of chocolates. I was pleased to be able to offer something now to Josephine. Catherine told me how she had spent the morning with Lorenzo explaining that she was not ready to accompany him back to Milan. He had been very insistent but she feared that all this rushing about was going to lead to disaster and insisted on taking her time. I didn't know how to respond because I was so pessimistic about the theatrical total renunciation she hoped for, so I chose to say nothing. Loving the same man one's whole life is, it must be said, an audacious project—and yet I had managed to do it, more or less. I believe the only way to save a marriage is to practice some sleight of hand to avoid the abyss of monotony. One must seek light within the darkness, color amid the gray. One must be creative, bold, and unflinching. One needs a sense of humor, of course, and a touch of derision, but also imagination and myth. One must have a gift for the fantastic.

I introduced my new friend to my daughter and Luna.

The doctor came by on his rounds and explained to each of us that we needed to stay a few more days to have further tests. I was rather put out by this news, but Josephine did not seem to mind very much. We organized our storage bins with Catherine and Luna looking on, and they offered to see right away about getting us a proper dinner.

When they returned, our disgusting food trays had already arrived. But Josephine simply repeated her disposal procedure of that morning.

"But why are you throwing all that away?" asked Catherine in horror.

"We're not going to eat that slop!" replied Josephine.

"But you don't need to flush it down the toilet! Why not just leave it on your tray?"

"To avoid upsetting them."

"But you're not going to upset them! It's absurd to throw out food."

And so it was that Catherine managed to harangue the only reassuring human being I'd met over the last twenty-four hours.

Josephine got back in her bed.

Luna offered her some potato chips and salted peanuts, which she readily accepted.

"Today you'll have to make do with what I found at the bar, but tomorrow we'll do a proper shop."

"Oh but this is great, really. Always better than that hospital slop! But tell me, Catherine, what are you going to do? Are you going to stay in Paris or return to Milan?"

"Luna has to go back Saturday, and I was thinking of staying one more week to think things over more."

"Well, do exactly what you think is best, my dear. Madame Joseph can shop for you if you give her a list."

"That's okay, but thanks. Luna and I are taking care of things."

After they left, Josephine and I watched television and chatted. We talked about our families. I made her laugh several times—something which always gives me enormous pleasure. Even at my age, I like laughing. And what's more amazing is that I manage to do it still. Gabriel was like me, but we didn't lack lucidity and realism. The softness of our childhood probably forged in us the conviction that no matter what happened there is always derision and laughter as a way of thumbing one's nose at tragedy. I would like to die laughing—that would be my triumph over this last humiliation, laughter as my ultimate rebellion. Josephine seemed to appreciate my old-lady insolence as coming from someone who has nothing left to prove, but more importantly I think she understood the painful underside of my ironic barbs. It was my way to remain standing during the storm, refusing to yield to adversity and to show my fears and sufferings.

Luna came to see me every day and stayed for several hours reading in a chair, oblivious to our light conversation.

"What are you reading?" Josephine asked her.

"A book for my thesis."

"And what's your thesis on?"

"The educational system invented by Rudolf Steiner."

"And who is Rudolf Steiner? I've heard that name, but I know nothing about him."

"A genius of sorts, but hard to define. He was a philosopher, pedagogue, esoteric, architect, farmer, doctor, and the founder of anthroposophy, biodynamic agriculture, eurythmy, Steinerian education, and Weleda products. Does that fill you in?"

"And you, Christiane, do you know him? I never read anything by him."

"Well, yes, by chance I do in fact, though I think in France not many people have heard of him, perhaps because he was Austrian."

"So what? Mozart was Austrian too."

"But in Steiner's day we weren't crazy about Germanic culture."

"And so how do you happen to know him?"

"Because I had an aunt who was a follower of his."

"By the way, Mamie, you have to explain something to me."

"What's that, dear?"

"Why did you tell me that Papyrus went to the Goetheanum, and later you told me that the only time he met Steiner was at the Munich lecture?"

"Because I didn't know whether to tell you what happened after."

"And why wouldn't you?"

"First because it's upsetting and second because it would reveal secrets that don't belong to me."

"And these secrets, they're still alive?"

"The secrets are still secret, yes, because I'm the only one who knows them. Those involved are all dead."

"And you're bound by some oath?"

"No."

"So what's the problem?"

"So we'll see."

"You know, about esotericism," interjected Josephine, "when I went to Indonesia, I saw the craziest thing."

"Oh really? What?" asked Luna.

"I saw with my own eyes a witch doctor remove a cyst from the shoulder of a man without using a knife!"

"What do you mean without a knife?"

"You might not believe me but the witch doctor was in a trance and the patient was sweating profusely like a sick person. The witch doctor placed his thumb on the cyst and moved it up and down and down and up, like that, and the cyst disappeared. I never understood how he did it."

"Well, I can see why you two get along so well!" Catherine chimed in with a knowing glance at Josephine and myself.

"Do you mean because we both have wild imaginations?"

"Well, let's say vivid imaginations."

"What does that have to do with anything?" asked Josephine, sincerely surprised. "I saw it happen and so did lots of other people. I'm not saying it's true, I'm telling you what I saw and that none of us could figure out how it had happened. Imagination has nothing to do with it. The power of suggestion, perhaps, but still it's super interesting."

"Well, to come back to our Steiner story, Mamie, I'd really like you to tell me what happened at the Goetheanum."

"Oh, I don't know."

"But what's the problem?"

"Listen, you know I'm not the overly sensitive type, but really, I'm not thrilled about telling you things that I know you're not going to believe."

"But if you tell the truth, we'll believe you," said Catherine.

"I'd be surprised."

"But me, I always believe you," said Luna. "You see things that others don't notice, that's all."

"Thank you dear, but you're just saying that to butter me up."

"No I mean it. Mom, it's true!" she said, turning to Catherine. "If you saw a pink elephant, you would say, 'What is that elephant doing in the garden?' and then later if someone said there was a pink elephant in the garden, you'd answer, 'What do you mean pink? Pink elephants don't exist!'"

"Yes, well, there your mother would be right. There are no pink elephants," said Josephine.

"Thank you, Josephine, for coming to my defense. I'm beginning to believe your story of the operation with no knife," added Catherine smiling.

"You're pretty when you smile, you know."

Chapter Fourteen

B ette had made friends with a Russian anthroposophist she met in Paris in 1920. The woman in question, Princess Natasha Bolinkova, was a distant cousin of the Czar who had fled the 1917 revolution in Russia. After the Munich lecture, Bette returned to Paris, where she spent the fall. Geoffroy joined her there as soon as he was able to. Papyrus was also in Paris with them sometimes, but he had begun courting my mother and therefore spent more time in Picardy.

For the Louvenel family, it was out of the question to allow Marguerite to go and spend time in Paris with her suitor, even with Bette as chaperone.

Papyrus probably set about modeling a more orderly life so as to merit his pious and orderly future spouse, but something tells me he must have found the process rather oppressive from the very beginning. I'm convinced that he went off to Paris now and then with the same eagerness for oxygen as someone coming up for air from the bottom of a deep swimming pool.

Bette's novel ways and her obsession with Steinerism must have been an exotic and amusing distraction from the psychological straitjacket of the Picardy aristocracy. Marguerite's idea of love was as romantic and idealistic as Papyrus was disenchanted and wounded underneath his boastful, gay exterior. He nevertheless did his best to go along at least partially with this romantic idyll that she seemed intent on living out. It was the biggest mistake of their lives.

The prevailing culture of the time favored my mother's view of things, and that is probably why he did everything he could to contain his demons without ever confronting them directly. He made no attempt to understand them and thereby control them. He simply pushed them down, as they yelled and shook their fists, into the cellar of his soul, and tried to cover over with good intentions all the vociferation and pestilence of his deepest anxieties.

One day in September, Bette, Geoffroy, and Papyrus met up in Paris.

Geoffroy and Papyrus were living as usual in the home of their aunt Gertrude, the mother of Cousin Vincent. She was rich and shameless but very lively and generous. She adored her nephews and detested any kind of boundaries. At fifty-five she would have been ridiculous in many settings, but she had an undeniably playful, juvenile charm that made her attractive and droll and preserved her from society's low meanness.

On a certain Friday, they had the surprise of Cousin Vincent's arrival. They were all happy to be reunited again. Elodie was also in Paris and staying with relations of hers. Vincent wanted to present her to his mother and it was decided to organize a dinner the next evening at the sumptuous residence of Aunt Gertrude in avenue Montaigne. Bette requested permission to invite her dear friend, the Princess Bolinkova, whom she had not seen for some time. That afternoon the three friends and Bette, Princess Bolinkova, and Elodie went to take advantage of the last rays of summer in the Bois de Boulogne.

They rented a little boat and rowed out to the restaurant that faced the lake and enjoyed cups of tea and a delicious raspberry tart. They seemed to be a happy and harmonious little band. Elodie was liked by all right away. She was rosy and plump, uncomplicated and kind, and laughed easily. She seemed surprised by nothing and to enjoy everything. The Princess on the other hand was quite different. There's no denying she was beautiful, in a catlike way, with prominent cheekbones and enormous, light, almond-shaped eyes. She was a bit odd, both captivating and disarming, but agreeable company all the same.

The young group then went down to sit closer to the shore. Vincent and Elodie amused themselves with attempts to splash each other.

"They look happy, don't you think?" asked Bette.

"I must say she has a lot of charm," Papyrus replied.

"Kind and a good character, that's what a soldier needs," added Geoffroy to tease Bette.

"The Princess has nothing to say?" asked Papyrus.

"I don't butt into other people's business. Besides, who can say what attracts two people. It's a marvelously intimate matter."

She made those remarks in a low voice while aiming her catlike eyes directly into the eyes of Papyrus. He held her stare more as a challenge than as a promise. Certainly the evening promised to be interesting.

When they had returned to the house after bringing the Princess back home, Bette said to Papyrus, "Natasha clearly likes you a lot. I'm jealous."

"A little jealous?"

"No, jealous. Don't think I'm going to modify my declaration with any quantifying adverb. 'A little' or 'very' would only be reductive, you know."

"Bette, quit these games, please."

He said that in one short breath while she retained a perky air. Geoffroy then came into the living room.

"Ah Geoffroy, I was just saying to Louis that I'm jealous of the interest that the Princess takes in him."

"Bette, my angel, you cannot have us all to yourself. You have to share a little."

He punctuated this admonishment with a little kiss on her pretty forehead.

It was then time to dress for dinner, so everyone returned to their rooms.

When they were reunited in the large salon, each holding the stem of a full champagne glass, Cousin Vincent announced his engagement to Elodie.

Aunt Gertrude applauded softly and threw a puzzled look in the direction of her future daughter-in-law. Was she disappointed that her only son was marrying a simple and kind young woman instead of one of those spoiled, libertine heiresses that she could have become friends with? Or was she merely thinking about the reasons for his choosing someone so far from the maternal model? Or wondering if she could ever put up with there being another woman in Vincent's life. Whatever the cause, Gertrude remained friendly and courteous but didn't show the overflowing affection that such circumstances would customarily elicit.

Elodie didn't give a damn, and with cheeks on fire laughed a toothy laugh in celebration of the happiness that lay ahead. I will jump forward to say that it was the best of marriages—they loved each other tenderly their whole lives and nothing ever stained the joy they had being together. Too bad for Aunt Gertrude—she would eventually get used to the idea that her son's pursuit of happiness had driven him to look for a woman who was totally unlike her.

During dinner, Geoffroy, who'd had a bit more to drink than some, requested everyone's attention.

"I too have a declaration to make. I raise my glass to the most fascinating woman in the world. Oops, sorry, Elodie, but I'm not talking about you. The woman who has bewitched me is named Bette and I have asked her to marry me."

Papyrus detested this sort of public display. He felt an unspeakable irritation toward this grandiloquent brother of his. But it was not the only reason behind his awkward smile and frozen stare. Of course everyone applauded, but Cousin Vincent, who wanted to be witty, inquired, "Yes, but what was her answer? Maybe she wants nothing to do with you!"

Bette glanced quickly at Papyrus and with a big smile responded, "Well, guess what? I accepted and soon I will have every right to call you Cousin Vincent."

"I'm very happy to hear that, my future cousin. But I don't know why I've always been 'Cousin Vincent' and never simply 'Vincent.'"

"Well, it's because you have the same name as your father, my dear," replied Aunt Gertrude. "It was to distinguish you from him. Would you have preferred we call you 'little Vincent'?"

"Given that he's six-foot-three, that name wouldn't have fit so well today," added Geoffroy.

Everyone except Papyrus was in good spirits. The general euphoria unsettled him, but not simply because of Bette, whom he was surely fond of. Papyrus's heart was too scarred for him to easily put up with scenes of gaiety. He found them mushy and affected. He had had moments of enchantment too, and he knew how rare and precious they were, which was probably why he did not exhibit them and instead tucked them down inside his coat like a thief.

The Princess never laughed that much and spoke in low tones — Papyrus liked that. She often gave him long looks which left no doubt in his mind that she was attracted to him.

After the dinner, Bette and Natasha sat down together away from the others.

"Bette, you must help me. I wrote to Rudolf Steiner asking to attend the Christmas conference at the Goetheanum."

"But that's great news! I will be there too with my dear Geoffroy. I couldn't be happier if you'll be there too."

"The problem is Steiner doesn't want me there."

"What are you talking about? Of course he wants you. Why are you having such crazy thoughts?"

"Because he said so in a letter."

"He wrote and told you he doesn't want you there?"

"Of course not. You know how he's always charming and courteous. He says there's no more room and he can't make any exceptions. He told me to come to the Easter conference, but that's too late."

"Nonsense, go at Easter! If you like I'll go with you. Really, Christmas or Easter, what difference does it make?"

"It's my last chance to see the Goetheanum."

"What do you mean by that, Natasha? You're worrying me terribly."

"We're going to lose the Goetheanum. At Easter it will no longer exist as you know it. And I, I've never seen it. The Goetheanum will burn down and there'll be nothing left of it."

"What are you saying?"

"I've had a premonition and I'm never wrong. The Goetheanum will go up in flames long before Easter."

"And you wrote to Steiner about that?"

"Of course."

"And what did he say?"

"He said he was not surprised. He told me that from the start of construction, Ahriman had been working against the project. He said that no sooner had the cornerstone of the building been set in place than the sky suddenly darkened, thunder claps rang out, and a furious wind kicked up. He understood this was a warning and then turned to the north, west, south, and east to announce to his disciples that this stone represented man's soul condemned to battle and that it was necessary to find the strength to resist Ahriman at all costs."

"Oh my dear Natasha, what you're telling me is truly frightening."

"Bette, help me to attend the Christmas conference, I beg you."

"I promise to do everything I can."

After everyone had dispersed, Papyrus and the Princess were alone together. After a moment she said, "You're not happy to see Bette with your brother, is that right?"

"Of course I am, what are you talking about? I love Bette very much!"

She said nothing more. He got up from his seat and sat down next to her. He pulled her close and kissed her. She responded with such enthusiasm to his overture that he felt obliged to say to her, "I too will be marrying Bette's sister-in-law."

"I know. Aristocrats always marry within their own circle, and it's a good thing too, really. But kiss me again."

The Princess proved to be quite keen. Without going into details, she was tireless and Papyrus had a wonderful time with her. There's no doubt that with my mother things were more sedate.

At Christmas Geoffroy came down with a bad case of the flu. A few days before they were scheduled to leave for Dornach, he was trembling with a very high fever. Bette objected to his accompanying her.

"Not only do you risk dying on the way, but you'll infect everyone there."

"I don't want you to go alone."

"Of course I'll go alone. Come on, Geoffroy, I'm sorry, but I'm not a child any longer."

"No, please, at least let Louis accompany you."

"Oh really, Geoffroy! I get along just fine with Louis, but he and anthroposophy are absolutely incompatible!"

"I'm not so sure. Really, he and I are not so different."

"What? You're totally different! You are kind and gentle. He is tense and volcanic."

"Yes, well, it will do him a lot of good to be plunged in all that spirituality."

"When you start mocking, you do resemble him, in fact."

"Let me ask him to accompany you, please."

To make a long story short, he ended up persuading Papyrus to accompany Bette to Dornach. He had no desire to go, but his brother made him do it.

"What's more, that crazy Bolinkova woman finally got herself invited and she's made some apocalyptic predictions."

"She's going to be there too?"

"I know, old boy, it's really a sacrifice I'm asking of you!"

"Quit joking! Can you see me alone with those two lunatics?

"Hey, watch your mouth! One of them is going to be my wife in three months and the other one you'd fuck in a flash, admit it."

"Fuck her? Are you fucking crazy? There in their sect's cuckoo's nest? That would indeed be a sacrifice you'd be asking me to make."

In fact all three of them were upset by this trip: Papyrus for the reasons he so elegantly formulated to his brother; Bette and the Princess because they considered Papyrus to be an erratic force disturbing their spiritual development. In any case he ended up joining them after Christmas in a rather rustic guesthouse in a German-speaking area very close to the Goetheanum, which was Bette's wish because she did not want to stay at her own home in Basel. Papyrus had clearly stated that he would not attend any lectures, and he was therefore getting ready to hunker down in this deserted place and in the worst weather of the year with only a pile of books he'd brought along to occupy him.

The night they arrived their host had prepared a decent meal that included a delicious cheese fondue and enough alcohol to lift Papyrus's spirits somewhat. Other guests ate in silence around them.

When they were alone, the Princess said to him, "Well, well, you must be really fond of your sister-in-law to spend so many days cooped up in your room reading and yawning."

"No, it's my brother I love and it's my brother who asked me to do it!"

"Yes, curious that he was so insistent."

"He wants to know she's not alone in that nuthouse of a sect that you also belong to, my beautiful and adorable friend."

"Oh, don't tease me, it's really not the moment for that."

"Why's that, because the spiritual retreat has already started?"

"And you prefer mockery instead of facing what's bothering you?"

"And what is it that you think is bothering me?"

"Bette is in love with you and you're too much of a rake not to have noticed."

"You're mad! Bette is in love with Geoffroy, otherwise why would she have agreed to marry him?"

"Did she really have a choice?"

The gaze of her light green eyes had a strange ambiguity—a sort of painful caress—but Papyrus was too agitated to notice. Bette then returned.

"This is such a darling little dining room, don't you think?"

"Yes, it's perfect."

"Louis, what will you do tomorrow? Won't you be bored out of your mind?"

"No worries. I'll get up late and go out walking. Really, don't worry about me. And besides, I've come prepared. I've got *War and Peace* in my bag. I'll never have a more perfect moment to get through it."

"Oh my poor dear, what a situation your brother's thrown you into."

The slightest wisp of a smile crossed Natasha Bolinkova's lips. Papyrus hated her.

The next morning, when he came down at eleven for breakfast, he was greeted like an alien. The owners were already preoccupied with the bratwurst and potato rösti that were to be served at noon. Papyrus waited with his book and then ate like an ogre. He spent the rest of the afternoon walking and then reading in his room until the ladies returned. The first few days went by smoothly like that, but then he did begin to get bored. He hired a car and driver and set off for Basel.

"Do you speak French?" he asked the driver.

"Naturally."

"There's no way of knowing. You're Swiss, right, so I should be speaking German. Well, I'm lucky to fall in with you since I only speak my mother tongue."

"Yes, and you're lucky it's French!"

"What do you recommend in Basel?"

"Walking around of course, and visiting the cathedral. I also advise you to buy some *bruns de Bâle*" — they're called *brunsli*."

"What are they?"

"Chocolate cookies with almonds and cinnamon. You can only get them at this time of year. *Läckerli* are also good. They're little gingerbreads with icing typically eaten at New Year's time — and they're as good as their name."

"What do you mean?"

"*Lecker*, that means delicious in German."

"Oh, I see. I'll be sure to buy some."

He had the driver drop him off at the cathedral, which he visited. Then he walked along the Rhine. The air was bracing and the day was bathed in the intense light of sun on snow. Papyrus thought to himself that things weren't going too badly. He ducked into a post office and sent off a postcard to Marguerite. It was not quite three p.m. when he stepped into a tearoom with a charming green facade situated along the river. He sat down at a little round table that faced a large Venetian mirror, and what to his wondering eyes should appear but the reflection of the face of the Count de Redan. At first he thought he was hallucinating, but no, the face in the mirror reading with concentration an English newspaper was without a doubt that of his old friend.

"Charles, you old scoundrel, what are you doing here?"

"I can't believe my eyes! And you, what brings you here?"

"Oh, this is the best thing that could have happened to me!"

"What? Being here?"

"No, this place is a sort of purgatory for me. I mean running into you, what good fortune! But you, what brings you here at the holiday season? And please, don't tell me you're leaving tomorrow!"

"Haha! You always made me laugh, Louis. I have no appointments, no schedule—it's one of the perks of being an old bachelor. And pardon me for saying so, but you completely underestimate the charms of this region. There are many marvelous things to see and visit. But will you have time?"

"I have all the time in the world."

Papyrus told the Count the reason for his being there. The Count remembered Bette well and her enthusiasm for anthroposophy. After Papyrus bought some *brunsli* and *läckerli* for Bette and Natasha, as well as for his driver, they went to the museum in the city center.

"No one recommended the museum to you, how can that be? You'll see works of Holbein from the Amerbach

Cabinet collection. They're really splendid! Your friends don't have a thought for anything down-to-earth!"

Papyrus blushed inwardly, thinking of his down-to-earth encounters with the Princess, but as he was a gentleman he simply made a silent nod of acknowledgment.

The museum was indeed rich in its holdings of works from the Middle Ages and the Renaissance, including some magnificent Strasbourg tapestries, but Papyrus stopped the longest before a series of engravings of a sort of Saint Vitus's dance with a group of skeletons on a tomb.

"You seem rather entranced," murmured Charles de Redan, coming up behind him.

Papyrus made no reply and continued his examination.

"It's known as a *danse macabre*, an allegorical motif of the Middle Ages representing the universality of death. The dead person buried, you see, might be a king or emperor or pope, but could just as well be a peasant or child. It's supposed to remind you of the precariousness of your existence and the inescapable triumph of death over vanity. Study it well, Louis, it can only help you with your boastful swagger."

"I was in the war, Charles."

At the end of the afternoon they said goodbye, but not before agreeing to meet again the next morning to visit Colmar together. When Louis arrived at the guesthouse around six p.m., the ladies were already waiting for him at the dinner table, even though he had been hoping to rest a bit first.

"Say, at what time do they eat, these Swiss?"

"Early," Bette replied laughing. "But they also get up early. Our poor host was very concerned about you this morning and wondered if he should knock on your door to see if anything was the matter."

"Well, tomorrow he'll have nothing to worry about, because I'm getting up at dawn to go to Colmar with you'll never guess whom."

"Whom?"

"Charles de Redan, my Paris friend."

"What a coincidence! And what is he doing here?"

"He says he's very fond of this region and is traveling alone. He showed me some very nice things in fact. Oh, by the way, I brought you some cookies."

"Oh, *läckerli*!" cried Bette, opening the box of cookies. "I love them. Taste this, Natasha. It's a typical food from around here at holiday time."

They ate heartily and drank a lot of white wine. They concluded their meal wrapped in their fur coats sitting on the wooden bench in the hotel courtyard. There they drank *pflümli* out of little crystal Bohemian glasses and ate more of the cookies Louis had bought in Basel. The crisp cold air gave a particularly sharp clarity to the starry night—a clearness only clouded by the regular puffs of water vapor from their mouths as they breathed.

"The night is so beautiful that it seems flat, like an immense black stole," said Natasha.

"Yes, let's stop breathing. We're staining it with our breath," murmured Bette.

"Bette, if we stop breathing, we'll die," said Papyrus. "Life always causes some stains, but that's life."

"Louis, look, those stars seem so close."

"I'm going to bed, my friends," said Natasha. "Tomorrow we're getting up early and finishing late. I have to ring out 1922 in top form." The Princess went back inside the hotel, leaving in her wake a slight scent of lavender and talcum powder.

"Louis, I've never yet thanked you for accompanying me because I thought it a bit odd. But I know you're rather bored and it bothers me to know you're by yourself and at loose ends. Plus, you're far from your young fiancée on account of me."

"Well, to tell you the truth, I was a bit worried about this whole thing too, but now I'm very happy with every bit of this escapade."

"You think we're two nutcases, don't you?"

"Everyone is trying to make sense of their lives. I don't judge you."

"And you, what sense have you made?"

"What do you see there?"

He asked Bette this question while raising his head to the night sky and taking her hand in his. Bette's little hand was so soft that he felt he would capsize. He told himself he should let go of it, but also that it was too late and that the poison was already coursing in his veins. He then repeated in a shaky voice, "What do you see there?"

"I see the immensity, but I also see a line which, extended to infinity on my right, arcs back to the starting point on my left. The starting point and the end point overlap eternally."

She leaned her head on his shoulder after drinking a sip of *pflümli*.

"And you, Louis, what do you see?"

"I see emptiness. An emptiness that's impossible to define and to avoid."

"Do you believe in God?"

"I only believe in matter now, Bette."

"But matter is made of spirit!"

"Matter is made of matter."

"You don't believe that yourself."

"I saw death triumphant dancing on faith, Bette. In the trenches, there was no more God, no more spirit, as you call it, but instead the awful, incommensurable triumph of matter. Mere kids who minutes earlier were writing to their fiancées, walking here and there to avoid going crazy, trembling with fear—they were eating, sleeping, reflecting. And then seconds later their bodies are blown to bits, a leg here, an arm over there. I came across a hand that had begun decomposing while still gripping the photograph of a woman."

"And yet you say they thought, they loved. You don't say their brain was thinking, or their brain loved. You know there is something that goes beyond mere anatomy."

"You're fooling yourself, Bette."

She raised her head to look at him. He had such an air of suffering that she no longer recognized him. He turned his head to her and there what had to happen happened—they kissed. In fact, they devoured each other. It was evident that the passion that expressed itself in their gestures originated far back, so far back that they did not see it coming. What remained of the *pflümli* tipped over into the snow, and tipping themselves, they gave themselves up to their furious ardor outstretched on the bench. Then they righted themselves. Papyrus took her hand and guided her back to his room. They made love wildly, brutally, as though their need to dissolve into each other was related to some old grievance; then they calmed down, they felt each other, caressed each other. That lasted a long time; they never seemed sated.

Chapter Fifteen

Two orderlies entered pushing a cart with our dinners on it. I stared at the trays in horror, but as soon as the orderlies left the room Josephine sprang from her bed to unpack our provisions. She handed me an open-faced cheese sandwich of *vache qui rit*, a yogurt, and a banana.

"There, that will tide you over so you don't starve, and later if you like I have some butter cookies."

"I'm being wonderfully spoiled, Josephine, thank you so much. Your cuisine is excellent!"

Luna and Catherine sat in silence.

"What are you thinking?" I asked them.

"About everything you've told us…It's crazy."

"It's not crazy, it's life, and when passion overtakes you, it totally takes over!"

"She really got around, your aunt Bette! She wound up doing it with the whole family!"

"Luna! No disrespect for your grandmother, please!"

"Oh Catherine, no! I like her frankness. She's not being disrespectful, simply spontaneous."

"Spontaneity is good. Me, I like spontaneous people," Josephine interjected while munching her sandwich.

"There are limits. We are after all talking about our own great aunt."

Wham! That was aimed at my Josephine to let her know *You're not one of us!* My friend got the message and looked back at Catherine perplexed. I think she was wondering where my daughter's aggressiveness came from. Catherine had absolutely no idea what it felt like to be excluded. She had always lived in a world where she was granted her place. In my life this had not always been the case. I recognized it immediately as soon as any group of people drew itself into a closed circle. I am wildly hostile to such behavior and feel like a hunted animal when I sense any form of exclusion happening. My whole life I've been the daughter of the pariah, of the debauched, miscreant drug user judged by a narrow world that only recognizes its own social codes. This is why I've always felt close to all minorities: the young against the old, the sick against the healthy, individuals against the masses, Indians against cowboys, and blacks against whites. It takes having lived that experience to know that the smallest drop of gratuitous hostility can create a chasm between you and the other person when fate has confined you within a certain singular position. I have experienced this painful feeling too often, like a sort of castaway in freezing ocean water, and am always terribly sensitive to it. Catherine could never have a sense of the invisible, gut connection that united me with Josephine, and for me at that moment it was my own daughter who was the stranger.

"I have nothing against Aunt Bette. Especially considering the time back then. It could not have been easy to do all she did," opined my dear Luna.

"You're not kidding!"

"And did you like her?"

"As a child I found her too sophisticated and especially the focus of too much adulation. So no, I couldn't warm to her. Besides that, Gabriel and I loved to spend time doing mock imitations of her dance steps with all those veils and exalted gestures."

"And then?"

"And then she saved my life."

"Really?" asked Catherine.

"Absolutely."

"But Mamie, how did it end between her and Papyrus?"

"It's a terrible story."

"*Oh là là!* What a soap opera!" said Luna. "But we're going to get kicked out now. Don't you tell any bits of the story without us, all right?"

"And what if I tell it twice," I replied with an impish wide-eyed stare back at Luna. "It's going to be hard to spend the evening together and not pick up the thread, right, Josephine?"

"No, no, we want to hear the first telling too! We don't want the warmed-over retelling! Please, you two!"

Mother and daughter left the room as the doctor was arriving on his rounds. I was just able to see Catherine take him aside as they quickly disappeared from my angle of vision. Luna came back and gave me a warm hug and kiss. She murmured that she loved me very much, and hearing that was like being lifted by pink butterflies. Then the doctor entered and she left. He began with me. He told me I had probably taken too many of my antihypertensive pills, perhaps accidentally double the normal dose, which is quite possible. He said I was fit as a fiddle, albeit an old fiddle, and that he would sign my release for the next day.

"As for you, Madame Morgel, we have ruled out any cardiac problem, and so you're free to go home tomorrow as well."

When we were alone I said to Josephine, "I'm sorry about what happened earlier."

"What do you mean?"

"My daughter was not very kind, but it was me she was really aiming at."

"But she loves you. She's constantly here!"

"Yes, but my daughter never really got the knack for life. You, you have it, I think."

Then she suddenly turned grave and serious.

"It's not easy. It takes discipline."

"And small pleasures. They bring a certain charm and are wonderfully helpful."

"It's true, they help."

"Yes, they do. Me, at my age, I always reserve a few daily doses of little things that please me. What do you do that makes you happy, and that's within reach, of course? Think of the simplest things, one mustn't be too demanding, either."

"Reading a good book, listening to music, walking around at flea markets with Mita my best friend. Drinking my coffee with milk in bed in the morning, putting on a new dress, finding a seat in the subway, watching the sunset at Place du Tertre, eating alone with my mother. And you? What are your pleasures?"

"For me eating with my mother was always a nightmare, and the Place du Tertre is too far away. Let's see...I know, watching a thunderstorm at Place Saint-Sulpice, looking out the window of my living room, having a whiskey while watching TV, smoking a cigarette at the end of a meal. Eating a whole seafood platter. All things that are harmful to me, I guess."

"And your family?"

"I love being with my daughter, even if she's a bit crabby, and with my granddaughter. The problem is they live far away, in Italy."

"One has to defend oneself by holding on to very simple things, because life is extremely complicated."

"And when it stops being complicated, when it loses its richness, which is also the source of the bumps and burrs, and its contradictions, when it's only a smooth plane, then life really stinks."

That night I had a lot of trouble falling asleep. I was thinking of Catherine, and I couldn't stop feeling as though I were somehow responsible for her sadness. A mother's sense of omnipotence is irrational, but it is true that we give life to our children. That's no small thing, therefore it's understandable that we puff ourselves up, and especially that we think even after they've left our womb that they're little pieces of our flesh that belong to us. Whereas in reality we've only ferried them across the uncertain river of existence, helping them pass from spirit to matter, as Aunt Bette would say. But it's also true that when they disembark, it's a little piece of our living flesh that goes out into the world. We owe them that at least, they didn't ask to be disturbed, that's for sure. So we can't complain, even if it hurts.

After watching a little television, we turned off the lights and continued talking for a while in our nearly totally dark room. Soon I sensed that my friend was answering less and less and falling asleep. But as soon as I stopped talking, she would pick up the thread. In fact she was doing what children do, she wanted to fall asleep while I told her a story.

Josephine's slow breathing, interrupted now and then by deeper breaths, gave me a tender feeling and yet I was also afraid. During the night in the hospital there are little sounds of light steps, metallic sounds of thermometers dropped in bowls and medicine bottles placed on trays. At night one hears sickness better. Doors open and close, letting silence circulate. A light green ray, impossible to extinguish, led me back to ancient fears. What I fear most in death is the solitude, because even without a soul and without consciousness, that stiff isolation crushes my heart. When Epicurus claimed that we never encounter our own death, it was the dumbest thing he ever said in his philosophical career. Life rests completely on this encounter.

Chapter Sixteen

I n the early morning hours when Papyrus opened his eyes and gazed at Bette's porcelain body caressed by the pale light of the moon, he did not feel remorse but rather a painful happiness. He did not think of Geoffroy, nor of my mother, nor of the terrible scandal that all of this would give rise to. He caressed her as in a dream where nothing real can interrupt pure desire. She opened her almond eyes and caressed his cheek. So she had not acted out of drunkenness. He read no sign of surprise in her beautiful features. She knew why she was there naked in Papyrus's bed.

"I'm going to return to my room and pretend nothing has happened. We'll be together again tonight after the lecture. Organize for us a fun New Year's party. I would like all of this to last all of next year, and the next, and the next one after that."

He was relieved to see that she was completely untouched by any feeling of regret. Later he went downstairs in a sweet euphoric state to have breakfast. He still smelled Bette's pulsing body under his hands and the scent of her skin. Papyrus was totally prostrate before this love, which I believe he had not really been conscious of before that day.

The weather was clear and cold again. The car was waiting to take him to Colmar where he was to meet up with the Count de Redan. Along the way, while he looked out on a snow-covered pine forest, behind which lay a succession of tranquil peaks and deserted valleys, the frost on his window held in place snow crystals as though trapped in a spiderweb. He put his nose up to the window to get a closer look. Each in its delicate beauty was a portion of the infinite.

Colmar is a beautiful small medieval town with narrow streets and lots of cute shops and brasseries. Many buildings in the center feature the characteristic Alsatian architecture with exposed wooden beams in latticework patterns. The Count de Redan was waiting for him at a table in a café on the main square.

"I propose we begin with a little walk around the city center, then we'll have lunch somewhere and finish with something quite extraordinary that I'll keep a secret."

"Why not begin with the surprise?"

"Because if we do that nothing else will seem worth your time."

"Sounds like a death knell."

"You must have a troubled conscience to say such things!"

The Count de Redan had a good laugh at his own joke, but Papyrus felt a little upset.

Papyrus thoroughly enjoyed the Count's company. Of all his friends, he was probably the most difficult to get a handle on. He was a worldly sensualist, but also solitary, educated, and loyal to the few principles he cared about. In fifty-plus years of life he had never married. It was often said that a horribly disappointing love affair had deeply marked him and led to his prolonged libertine bachelor-hood. Under a swashbuckling exterior, therefore, it was generally supposed that the Count de Redan was at heart a wounded romantic.

While they were dining on their sauerkraut and draft beer, Papyrus asked if he would like to come and celebrate New Year's Eve with the ladies, and the Count was happy to accept.

"But tell me, if it's not indiscreet, you're interested in the Princess, I suppose?"

"No, not in the least."

"Ah, well, that doubles my motivation to join you for this New Year's celebration then."

"Don't make any trouble for me. The Princess is damn pretty, I'll grant you that."

"And yet she doesn't interest you?"

"Not anymore."

"Pardon me. My poor Louis, I simply hoped that amid all this gentlemanly chaperone work you would have found yourself some modest compensation, but no! I really feel for you, old boy. But if you're not too overwhelmed by all these distractions, I assure you that you'll be deeply moved in your soul. This is my treat, by the way. Don't be silly now and follow me."

They went back out into the freezing cold and walked in the direction of the Musée Unterlinden. When they arrived at the heart of the museum church, the Count said in a voice trembling with excitement, "Here is something that you will never forget — the Isenheim Altarpiece."

At first, Papyrus was unable to take in the sumptuous grandeur of the polyptych. He was not very cultured and he thought this was merely one more example of scenes of the Crucifixion that can be found in many churches.

"All these panels that you see were painted in the early sixteenth century by Matthias Grünewald. The panels articulate out and reveal this central area of sculptures by Nicolas de Haguenau. It's called the Isenheim Altarpiece because it comes from the monastery of Saint Anthony in Isenheim, not far from here. Now we can just look on in silence if you like."

Papyrus walked around the panels while taking care not to stick too close to his friend, for he saw that the Count was overcome by deep and strong emotions just then. He tried therefore to be discreet and respectful while at the same time giving some thought to why the Count might be so absorbed in contemplation of this work of art. He began by studying the Crucifixion and the Deposition of Christ. Something infinitely powerful emanated from these images. Jesus's bony tense hands posed against the wood attracted his attention. He stared at them intently. Mary in a white robe that looks like a shroud is on the verge of fainting. John the Baptist's know-it-all pose irritated him, but on the whole the representation threw him into a state of high anxiety. He continued his examination of the piece with increasing attention. As he was contemplating a hermit being attacked by horrible monsters, he heard the Count's voice behind him: "This is Saint Anthony entangled with his demons, so you understand why this painting speaks to us so powerfully."

"You believe in sin then, Charles?"

The Count did not answer and walked away. Papyrus sat on a bench and continued to gaze at Saint Anthony and the monsters while thinking about the question he had asked his friend. The fact that the Count didn't suspect that he could feel any attraction for his sister-in-law proved that he had thereby committed a worse fault than a depraved person could imagine.

Saint Anthony, lying on his back and undergoing the assault of a number of abject, well-fed creatures, has the face of a terrified, defenseless child. This scene certainly incited belief in sin.

The memory of Bette's skin returned to him along with a light shiver. He imagined himself in the place of Saint Anthony helpless underneath Bette as succubus, an expression of ravishment on her face, wild with mouth open, and he felt uncomfortable. He thought again about all that Walpurgis Night stuff and how Bette had so often spoken of it in relation to Rudolf Steiner. What if all of a sudden everything stopped and his soul was ripped from his body and he found himself in the company of Mephistopheles in the spiritual world? What would still be on his mind is Bette's body, not Geoffroy's disappointment and suffering. Sin was located there, in his total abdication, the total surrender of his standing as a man, brother, and friend. There's the sin, the look of incredulity in the gaze of the person cheated and cast aside, and there's the indelible mark of passion that erases everything including the person we really are. But it's our conscience that makes us guilty, thought Papyrus, and not so that we collapse into abject resignation without the least resistance.

"Saint Anthony is sinning because he's struggling," he murmured.

"No, old boy, don't try to sugarcoat it. It's not by ignoring our own abject behaviors that we can ever avoid the torments of conscience."

"You are a merciless old fellow, my dear Charles."

"And you are too condescending toward us."

"And what if I were worse than you?"

"I'd find that surprising, but why not?...It's beautiful, isn't it?"

"Very beautiful. You were right to have our visit conclude with this wonder. The only bit that I dislike is John the Baptist with his finger-pointing. Don't you find his pose somewhat self-righteous-looking?"

They arrived in Dornach in the late afternoon. The young ladies were still at the Goetheanum listening to a last Steiner lecture in a series devoted to "The Spiritual Communion of Humanity." Papyrus and the Count used the time to plan out a more luxurious New Year's Eve feast. They ordered the best available wines to be opened, and supervised decorating the table with pinecones and sprigs of holly. Charles de Redan reserved a room for himself and they both retired to take a rest. Bette and Natasha eventually returned with pink noses and frozen hands. They went up to change and came down again to the small salon thirty minutes later. They then all had some champagne and ate some petits fours with sausage prepared especially for that evening. The two women were delighted to rediscover their friend Charles de Redan and everyone had a very pleasant time over the course of the meal.

Papyrus and Bette, however, mostly avoided looking at each other. Papyrus felt safe in this parallel world at the table—there wasn't the least friction with his past life, the only link between all that and the present was Bette, and that gave the moment they were living the aura and lightness of a dream. When one was speaking, the other kept eyes lowered. All of this mutual evasion ought to have alerted the suspicions of Charles and Natasha, but they too were probably allowing themselves to be gently rocked by a spirit of euphoria with no sense of time or limits. Papyrus was waiting for the moment when he'd be alone in his room and Bette would come knock on his door. He knew she would be even more daring than the night before and that the limited amount of uninterrupted time they could spend together would make them even more desperately happy. He enjoyed waiting in anticipation of all this.

Fire engine sirens resounded in the starry, snowy night. Papyrus and the others heard them and were startled. Dornach was a tiny village and everything that happened was of general concern.

"Louis, go ask our host what's happening," said Bette nervously.

Louis stood up and went off to meet the hotel owner just as he was coming back inside looking very upset.

"What's going on?"

"The Goetheanum!"

"What about the Goetheanum?"

"It's on fire!"

"Oh my God!"

"I'm going there. Do you want to come with me?"

"Yes, but wait, I have to let the others know."

Papyrus went back half running to the dining room, where the two women gave him a worried look. No one knows what was going through their heads but it's certain that both already sensed some disaster was unfolding. Natasha, looking pale as a sheet, then burst out, "Bette! I told you this would happen! Do you remember my premonition?"

At that point Papyrus was seriously troubled because he also remembered, and he hated to acknowledge the notion that we can receive messages in any other way than by purely material communication!

They all put on their coats and went outside to follow their host up the hill. What they saw looked less worrisome than what they had feared. The west-facing wall was totally destroyed and the interior of the structure was in flames, but long hoses were already in position and spraying the fire with heavy flows of water. Men had climbed onto the terrace and the fire seemed as if it would soon be under control. The firemen of the area had been quickly assisted by hundreds of men and women. Papyrus and Charles de Redan joined in offering their help. The smoke from the southern wing of the building did, however, continue to thicken.

Papyrus and other men hurried into the room of the great cupola, but they were met by the growl of flames that lashed out from between the walls. They attempted to save whatever they could by forming a human chain that included Bette and the Princess at the end of it. Charles de Redan couldn't stop coughing as the smoke got worse and worse. Bette realized he was not well and rushed to help him. The smell was intolerable, but Papyrus and the others battled to put out the flames, which raged higher. When Charles seemed to be suffocating, Bette, with the help of a few men, managed to bring him outside. A forceful man's voice relayed the order from Rudolf Steiner to abandon the building, but no one paid attention and they continued their labors until they were exhausted. Papyrus attempted still to do the impossible and despite the cries from the others continued his battle against the enormous fire. But he also eventually felt short of breath and had to turn back. No sooner was he out of the building than the two wooden cupolas crashed to the ground. A clock struck midnight and the year 1923 was born.

Rudolf Steiner ran about in all directions encouraging the men to abandon the fight. He didn't want to see anyone harmed. The lawn was filled with sculptures that he had set out for a production of *Faust*, so they were saved. Lying on the grass, his head resting on Natasha's knees, Charles de Redan was recovering slowly. Papyrus, seized by the idea that she was in some danger, was looking for Bette. In the distance he saw a woman's silhouette that he thought was hers, but it was an old woman with gray hair; then she turned and he saw that it was her. He was deeply startled.

"Bette, my poor Bette, what's happened to you?"

She broke down sobbing and threw herself into his arms like a child.

"Louis, Louis, they're going to kill him. They've already set about killing him. He's so good, so generous, Louis. I'm so afraid. And you, my poor Louis, you're all burned. You must have your burns looked at. Look at the palms of your hands."

In fact Papyrus had felt nothing. He was coughing a lot but felt no pain whatsoever. He held her against his chest and let her cry. They remained like that, holding each other, as the spectacle of the fire raged on. The insidious and hypnotic dance of Ahriman had managed to overcome the last pieces of resistance — everyone now looked on feeling conquered and resigned.

A single shadow could be seen among the ruins of the Goetheanum, the shadow of Rudolf Steiner, sad and silent, contemplating his work reduced to cinders. Papyrus deeply pitied this reserved man with his intelligent and good-natured demeanor. He'd only crossed his path twice, and each time in a perilous situation. Why was it that he found him so unsettling? Steiner approached them like a phantom. Bette straightened and held out her arms to him. He kissed her gently.

"Lots of work and long years," he said.

He delicately pulled away from Bette's hug and walked away in silence. His spectacles dangled from a piece of string. He was slightly stooped over.

As the sky lightened in the east, the men withdrew to their homes. Steiner let it be known that the conference would continue: "We will continue to accomplish the inner work we have yet to do in the premises that are still available to us. I will wait for you in the woodshop."

Papyrus, Bette, and the others returned to the inn exhausted. The look of their faces and hair covered in ashes caused them to smile in spite of themselves.

Papyrus was not very sophisticated, or perhaps he was overly sophisticated, but in any case he understood that it was now time for his love for Bette to end and with it all his loves.

He accompanied her back to her room and softly closed the door behind him. She did nothing to make him stay.

Chapter Seventeen

Luna often listens to a song that says, "Drink for thirst,
I don't know." I like that line. I like the whole song.
Luna has countless songs stored on a little device smaller
than my identity card. She places it on this pink thing that's
like a stereo.

I can still remember vinyl records and how we were
so worried about scratching them. I hear they've become
fashionable again—what don't you see if you live long
enough! Still, I think that music and books should take
up some space and not just exist in "virtual reality," as
one hears repeated every day now. They should be seen,
touched, smelled. I hate this absence of material stuff
between books and us today, and I always detested platonic
love affairs.

When one enters a room filled with shelves of books or
records, one feels at home, in an imperfect but warm environment of dust and diverse sensations. To open a book,
turn its pages, inhale its odor if one is alone—what an
exquisite bundle of sensations. Besides, love must be seen.
The Romans understood this when they invented marriage. Love must be shouted from the rooftops, exhibited

to all — marriage for us humans and libraries for books and records.

But the world is going in the opposite direction. One day, perhaps, if we're not careful, we'll have little pills of Tolstoy or Dostoyevsky. I can see the bookseller in her white pharmacist's coat: "*Chère Madame*, for your insomnia I'm prescribing a box of *War and Peace*. Take my word, you'll no longer feel the weight of those sleepless nights." Or "But Madame, short stories are only available in liquid form now. Munro? Here it is in red currant-blueberry flavor. Watch out for Edgar Allan Poe, however — it's important to never swallow him at night, especially if you have insomnia problems."

I arrived in Milan one July afternoon because Catherine insisted that I come visit. As planned, she patched things up with Lorenzo and for the moment everything was going fine, she said. Until the next time.

Josephine brought me to the airport. We arrived at Charles de Gaulle three hours early, because we're the kind of people who don't travel often and I was rather worked up about being late and keeping the schedule straight in my head and all this made me timid and nervous. Josephine, rolling my suitcase, bumped into a woman with flashy hair and the two of them burst out laughing and fell into each other's arms.

"What a surprise, Josephine. It's been such a long time!"

"It sure has! What a surprise indeed!"

"You don't know how many times I tried to track you down, but every time I came up empty."

"Do you still live in Berlin?"

"Yes, but I plan on moving back a few months from now. I miss Paris, you know."

Since they were clearly so delighted to have finally met up again, I suggested to my friend that I would just get in line on my own while they continued their conversation. When it was my turn at the check-in counter, I glanced back nervously at Josephine and gestured. She gestured back to tell me to go ahead and get started while she said goodbye to her friend.

"Are you checking any bags?" asked a young man who I could tell immediately had no problems of self-esteem.

"Uh, yes, my friend is bringing them."

"And where is your friend?" he asked with the unctuous affectation of one who is pleased to see you having a hard time.

"She's over there. She'll be right over. Can you begin by assigning me my seat?"

"Where over there?"

"Right next to your colleague who is directing passengers into the line." (Why the heck did I feel so unsure of myself in front of this arrogant little twerp?)

"Do you mean the black or the redheaded lady?"

"Do you mean the redhead or the black lady?"

"That's what I said."

"No."

"Yes."

"No."

"Look, if you don't have your luggage with you, you're going to have to step aside and wait for your friend and let me help the next person behind you, okay?"

"Yes, but in the time it takes for you to assign me a seat and check my passport..."

"Here I am, excuse me! Should I put it on the scale?" asked Josephine, slightly winded from her rush to get to the counter.

"Mm-huh," said the young jerk in an overtly unpleasant tone of voice. "And then step aside, Madame, you can see you're in the way, can't you?"

"But you haven't given me my boarding pass yet."

"But you're not the one I'm talking to, I'm talking to your friend!"

"But I need her. Don't worry, Christiane. I'll wait for you right here behind the barrier."

She rolled my suitcase to me and walked away. I was furious. I had been annoying to this little creep, there was no doubt about that, but Josephine had nothing to do with it, and in banishing her so brutally he had awakened in me all the horror and fury I feel when confronted with boorish, mean behavior—stupidity with its bull's forehead, as Baudelaire put it.

"Here's your boarding pass. Your plane will begin boarding at 3:30 p.m. at Gate B30."

I rejoined Josephine still trembling with rage.

"As friendly as a prison door, that guy," said Josephine smiling.

"Not another word about him, please. Come on, let's go have lunch. We have plenty of time."

While passing again in front of the airline employee who was directing passengers according to their flight destination, I noticed a friendly-looking burly man wearing a green T-shirt on which was written FUCK YOU. I considered it rather an odd choice to walk around with those words pasted on one's chest.

The man noticed my surprise and gave me a big smile and I did the same.

"I don't know who you are but you look nice," I said to him.

"Thank you."

"Could I ask you to do me a small favor?"

"If I can, why not?"

"If by any chance you end up at counter number five—do you see the young blond kid there?—would you be so kind as to thrust out your chest and let him know that I sent you?"

Josephine and the man in the green T-shirt had a good laugh, but I had hardly cooled down at all from the white-hot anger that had overtaken me.

When we left the hospital, we had exchanged telephone numbers probably with no real intention of seeing each other again. And then, one day, it occurred to me to go visit her at her bookshop. She was alone, sitting on a stool, immersed in her reading—*The Heart Is a Lonely Hunter*, by Carson McCullers, as it happens. When she looked up, I first thought she didn't recognize me; but she explained right away that it was just because she'd been totally absorbed in her book. And then she was so pleasant. Afterward everything was so easy and relaxed between us and we got in the habit of seeing each other regularly. I don't know what she sees in an old lady like me, but I think she's as fond of me as I am of her.

After our lunch, Josephine accompanied me as far as she could. Once we got to the security area we hugged and said goodbye as though we were never going to see each other again.

Catherine was waiting for me at Milan's Linate Airport. She looked elegant in a pair of matching white linen pants and top. She welcomed me with a big smile that gave me a warm feeling. I wondered how long it would take before she started feeling annoyed by me again. When had I started bothering her? Probably during her teenage years, as with every adolescent girl in the world—I know nothing about boys. For me it was different because my mother never interested me, whereas Catherine loves me, I'm sure of that. I must have disappointed her and that's the most painful feeling. Disappointing you, my child, is not falling from Olympus like a goddess condemned to a mortal's life and death. Disappointing you, my dear daughter, my love, is dying from disgust at myself knowing that the day will come when you'll pardon me. I know this because sooner or later you will come to find out how difficult it is to free oneself of the family legend that children write about us. For Pete's sake, Catherine, stop judging me. Stop waiting with your clipboard and sharp pencil as I forget my turn signal or make other mistakes and simply accept the love I feel for you for what it is.

Quite frankly I'm rather happy to be in Milan. Catherine and her family live in a lovely apartment across from the fine arts museum, the Pinacoteca di Brera, where I spend several hours every afternoon. It's a beautiful neighborhood that made me take back many of the negative preconceptions I had about Milan. We've already established our habits, which for me is the same as building one's nest, because at my age habits constitute my true home. In the morning I go out walking with my daughter and accompany her as she does the shopping. We then have lunch with Luna when she's free. In the afternoon Catherine has her things to do and I have mine. I often go to the museum. It never bores me to see the same things over and over. Besides, the museum has a rich collection and I walk slowly.

In the evening, Lorenzo returns and we drink good wine together. He's cheerful and charming. I also find him handsome, even elegant. He is so considerate that I start thinking he might actually like me. He has impeccable manners with my daughter, but that of course is not necessarily a good sign. One Sunday when he and I happened to be alone in the living room together he asked me if I wanted to spend the month of August with them in Tuscany. I told him that honestly I didn't think that was a good idea, that I would not at all enjoy feeling like I was becoming a burden, and that the good relations we enjoyed came in part from the fact that we saw each other very infrequently. He laughed and his beautiful teeth sparkled: "But I could never tire of you."

"That's nice of you to say, Lorenzo. As seducers, we know how agreeable that is to hear and how advisable it is not to believe it."

"But I do believe it."

"You don't know how bothersome I can become. Besides, why are you so intent on having me with you during your vacation?"

"Because you make everything more light and pleasant."

"Where are your women?"

"Luna and Catherine told me they would be coming back a little later than usual. Would you like a glass of wine while we're waiting?"

"You know I'm always up for that."

He got up and disappeared into the kitchen and soon returned with two wineglasses and a bottle of Brunello di Montalcino. His gestures were both relaxed and precise. He sat down, took a swallow, and then served me. I had the feeling he was searching for a topic of conversation and I was a little uncomfortable. Lorenzo speaks excellent French with an accent that is full of the southern sun.

"You see, I was wondering..."

I was wrong, he did know what he wanted to talk about but had been having trouble launching into it. I was now even more uncomfortable. He tried the intro again and began in earnest.

"I was wondering if you held anything against me."

I was perplexed.

"I mean if you're upset that I made your daughter suffer."

"Uh..."—I cleared my throat—"uh...well, frankly I don't believe it's any of my business, even though of course I'm sorry to see Catherine in such a state."

"So you are mad at me? I would consider that entirely normal."

"In fact, Lorenzo, it's more complicated than that. Naturally when there's trouble I just want to strangle you with my own hands, but as soon as you two make up I don't hold on to any resentment. Do you know why?"

"No, why?"

"Because I have always had a certain compassion for you."

"Is that so!" He lowered his head laughing. "You are really unsparing!"

"No, you've misunderstood me. I'm not being sarcastic or contemptuous. I feel a tenderness for you, for the war you're waging to save your love from your demons, for the storm and stress that overcomes you when what you consider to be a mere sideshow becomes a wrecking ball for the woman of your life. It's said that jealousy and love are two different things, but in the life of a couple I'm not so sure. I think they are intimately related within the megalomania of the lovers' project. If you cheat on your wife, in a way you betray the novel that you had intended to write together. I'm not judging you, and I repeat, nothing is more megalomaniac than to decide at a young age to desire the same person for the entire length of your long life, but I understand how she could feel trampled on by your horsing around."

He was my son-in-law and I was determined to defend Catherine, so I didn't want to seem too understanding. It wasn't an accident if my seductive son-in-law was drawing me out on this question—he was seeking my benediction. And that, my man, I won't give. Cheat on my daughter, fine, but feel all the pain that your guilt makes you endure. I'm not going to be the one to dress your wounds. I couldn't care less about tidy moralisms, but war is war, and what side I'm on is clear and you know it.

He didn't dare look at me anymore. He murmured about how sorry he was, that none of it was of any importance to him, that he let himself get carried away by certain light circumstances, and that paradoxically it strengthened his love for Catherine.

"Yes, of course. You know what Balzac said about this, don't you? If women only knew how much we love them by the evil that we do to them. Fine, but he does speak of the 'evil' that is done to them."

"Great, I have Balzac for a lawyer."

"Lorenzo, I suggest we talk about something else. This is very uncomfortable for me and for you too."

"You're right."

"I like you, but I'm not the person you can talk these things out with."

"Yes, pardon me. It's been very improper of me."

"It doesn't matter. Let's talk about vacations. I plan on spending two weeks at Saint-Briac."

"All by yourself?"

"No, with my friend Josephine."

We heard Luna's key turning in the lock. She was coming back from the movies. Catherine was soon back too, greeted us, and then went to the kitchen to prepare some pasta and a salad.

The conversation with Lorenzo had been rather irritating and kept me up that night. The window in my bedroom looked out on an interior courtyard. I opened the shutters to see if the moon was visible. Its light barely reached me at all.

The wide gateway opened noisily and a woman's silhouette crossed the courtyard in rhythm with the loud tapping of her heels. There was something eternal about this scene—it could have been from a hundred years ago, or two hundred, or more.

A woman crosses a courtyard with powerful strides, leaving to the night the memory of her little race to the light.

Nothing ever really changes.

Chapter Eighteen

F amilies have their secrets—those that end up being
discovered and those that cause behaviors, reactions,
and aptitudes whose origin will never be grasped. I don't
believe that everything is conditioned by what each generation hands down, but I will never stop believing that both
sufferings and dreams are passed on to the children and that
one should seek to limit the damage done.

And then there's also the unspeakable general state
induced by the overly close proximity of horror or
enchantment. By unspeakable I mean, for example, what
I feel inside when I put my arms around Papyrus's waist,
or the wind in my hair riding on his motorcycle. Gabriel
preferred being in the sidecar and that suited me fine. He
too was totally happy on those occasions—I saw it in his
eyes staring at the road and his little tight-fisted hands held
out in front. I knew the completely blank expression on his
face was in fact the expression of total bliss. A vertical line
between his eyes would invariably appear as soon as we left
the forest and rejoined the path that led back to the château.

Papyrus and my mother ended up marrying one year
after Bette and Geoffroy. Vincent and Elodie were the first

to go down the aisle. My mother had a lot of trouble getting pregnant and it would be three years before Gabriel was born. I followed two years later.

My earliest years were wonderful. My father was not that young anymore. He was thirty-six when I was born, but still very energetic and creative. He never let his sad, complicated side show in public. On the contrary, outwardly he always seemed cheerful and enterprising. He organized magnificent parties, became enthusiastic easily, and spent a lot of his free time making us merry in various ways. I didn't like horses and I gradually left that activity to Gabriel. In other areas, I was quite the terror and rarely failed to live up to my reputation. My mother totally gave up trying to tame our wild spirits, probably so that she could avoid Papyrus's criticisms. I remember once we rigged up a taut rope almost ten feet off the ground and pretended we were circus performers on the high wire. My mother came into the yard with her arms in the air and ordered Gabriel to get down from there.

"Oh be quiet! You're going to make him fall with all your yelling!" Papyrus interjected with a rather harsh tone of voice.

"Fine, you're in charge," she replied in a huff and returned to the house.

This little incident is a perfect example of how things were at my house: my mother had more or less abandoned us to his care. She was probably resigned to getting only the occasional half smile and "Yes, Mother," which masked our eagerness to stay away from her.

When Henriette, the cook, left us we were all very sad. She had always been there, even before we were born, and Papyrus was very fond of her; but she caught a bad case of the flu and died only a few days later. She was buried in the château's cemetery. It was the first funeral that my brother and I attended. She was replaced by a sweet young plump woman named Jeanne. Jeanne was always happy and laughing in a way that caused her large pink breasts to gently jiggle up and down and make us share in her joy. She was especially fond of Gabriel, who took advantage of her kindness to sneak off with large slices of cake. I wasn't jealous though, because she was also kind to me.

At the village school we were looked on as two inoffensive dunces. Gabriel had a certain cachet with the schoolkids, whereas I went mostly unnoticed. My admiration for Isabelle was not enough to get me to work harder. Her presence at least made me pretend to have done my homework, when I usually hadn't, and be attentive during lessons, when in fact I had a hard time concentrating. While our teacher, Madame Valence, was explaining to us the difference between the *passé simple* and the *passé composé*, all kinds of things were going through my head: Would I be able to steal a baby rabbit and hide it in my room without getting caught? How did the plumber's daughter manage to have so many warts on her hands and was I in danger of catching them? Where could Gabriel have left the copy of *Grimms' Fairy Tales* that he'd lost? My mind was racing in a thousand directions but never in the direction of what we were supposed to be learning. "Christiane, your head's in the clouds!" Madame Valence would say without any real severity in her voice. For her it was simply a statement of fact, my head was always in the clouds. The sentence was practically a weather bulletin.

At recess things went a bit better, but the king of the playground was definitely my brother.

Sunday school was worse, but that was because of my mother. She lectured me so much about how important it was to behave correctly with Abbé Chablet that whenever I had to appear before him I trembled from fear and did any number of silly things. I was concentrating so much on not making mistakes that I couldn't pay attention to anything and took terrible notes during his lessons. Abbé Chablet would scrutinize me, pleased to have a ready victim, while his large head and beard bobbed up and down. Everyone said what a good man he was, but I always found him to be a terrible phony and rather sadistic. Mother's praise for him never ceased, his religious title was enough to make him untouchable in her eyes.

Bible study was really torture for me. Gabriel was even more opposed than I was, but not for the same reasons. His smugness made him totally impermeable to the Abbé's lessons. It's true I was super shy. It took several dramatic incidents for me to become the old warrior I am today. But I was courageous and a small matter grew into an all-out war between the Abbé and me.

Madame Valence had assigned us lessons on syllogisms and I found myself very motivated by that topic. It was a reassuring form of clear reasoning for a wavering, doubting soul like myself. One just had to be sure of one's starting point, then the predicate, and the solution arrived with infallible force. I got into the nasty habit of creating syllogisms all the time. Abbé Chablet enjoyed emphasizing his words on the blackboard with forceful inscriptions in white chalk. This took place in a sort of garage-turned-Sunday-school classroom off the sacristy. God is your father. God is perfect. While he was going on about God's love and perfection, I'd be scribbling in my notebook: Papyrus is my father, Papyrus is perfect, therefore Papyrus is my God. I knew that something was not quite right in my syllogism, and that the link between the major premise and the minor premise was a bit shaky. While I was beating my brains to hit on the irrefutable proof of Papyrus's perfection, Abbé Chablet silently came up to where I was sitting. I can still see his face and the snarl of the meat-eating predator before the poor lost lamb. With one violent gesture, he snatched my notebook, and after reading what I'd written he burst out laughing.

"Listen to this, it's priceless: 'Papyrus is my father, Papyrus is perfect, therefore Papyrus is my God.' Amazing! You're lucky to have a champion of formal logic here in the classroom with you!"

It's well known that the group is always ready to be herded by the pastor. Everyone there echoed the Abbé's laughter, and not simply to please him. There was that inevitable satisfaction of having escaped the pillory oneself and the morbid attraction of witnessing the mortification of someone else.

I understood two things that day: first, that any form of intellectual dishonesty would drive me to a sense of failure;

and second, that in the future I would never force my brain to justify the blocked wellsprings of my heart. I would always cultivate clear thinking and my lucidity would be always merciless without seeking to do harm. I owe these character traits to Madame Valence's lessons on syllogisms and to the shaming inflicted by Abbé Chablet.

I was able to put up with the general mockery fairly well until I saw that Isabelle was also laughing along with the rest, displaying all her beautiful white teeth while rocking back and forth in her chair. That was too much for me. My throat tightened to the point where it was like the worst sore throat and large tears started streaming from my eyes as I fell apart sobbing convulsively.

The village doctor's daughter, Pascale Dagnan, had Down syndrome and was always seated next to me. She gave me the sad look of one who has experienced the cruelty of the wolf pack when it feels its superiority. She slid her hand into mine and I held tight to it with all my might.

The other thing I understood about myself that day was that I am capable of doing terrible, terrible things if I sense that they correspond to a group's general expectation. Everyone was expecting me to cry, and I cried. That perverse link unites me with others.

On the other hand, my fear of the Abbé had turned totally into visceral hatred. He would see what it meant to cross me.

The occasion presented itself one early afternoon in May when I went to confession. It was unseasonably hot and the Abbé was in the middle of digesting his lunch. I could hear him yawning and answering in an increasingly distracted, sloppy way. Suddenly his big head fell against the metal screen of the confessional box and I saw he was fast asleep. Such a lucky opportunity was unlikely to ever happen again and I sprang into action to make the most of it. A few hairs of his long beard protruded through the openings of the screen. I gently took hold of them and braided them together into a tight knot. As I skipped out of the church, I heard Abbé Chablet calling loudly for someone to come liberate him. I have no idea how he got free, but I think he was rather ashamed of that incident because he soon cut off his beard and he never ever spoke of my prank in public.

Gabriel was rather proud of me: "For once I really have to take my hat off to you. Unless you made this all up, that is."

"I swear it's all true. I ran off and he was screaming as though the devil were after him."

"Okay, well, let's hope it's true because it's really quite a feat you pulled off there!"

"I swear it's true," I said again, raising my right hand.

"Okay, okay, I believe you."

Already back then I had to fight for others to believe me.

Our mother glided through our lives like a shadow. One night I had a horrible nightmare and ran into her bedroom trembling. She was very kind and accompanied me back to my bed: "Wait for me here, honey, I'll be right back."

"No, I don't want to be alone."

"I'll be right back, I just want to get my holy water."

She disappeared and came back a few minutes later holding a carved Christ figure and a vial of holy water. She poured a few drops of the water on her index finger and made the sign of the cross on my forehead while holding the crucifix in her left hand.

"There, my dear, we've chased the devil from your room. He will no longer bother you because he fears Jesus Christ our Savior, who from now on will guard your sleep."

The poor woman meant well, but her story of Satan sneaking into my room terrorized me. Especially since she returned every night armed with her crucifix and holy water. From my bed I saw her phantasmagoric shape approach while I pretended to be sleeping. She made the sign of the cross over me while murmuring a prayer and then slipped out without making a sound.

My mother liked Elodie. She found her to be kind and pleasant company. She never displayed her antipathy toward Bette, on the contrary. One day when it was just the three of us at the table because Papyrus was at his garrison, my mother announced that Aunt Bette would be visiting in the afternoon.

"Oh no, not her!" said Gabriel.

"What do you mean, 'not her'?" replied my mother with surprise. "I forbid you to speak rudely about your aunt!"

"But what do you care? She's not your sister!"

"First, she was my sister when she was married to my brother before he died. Second, she is my sister-in-law, and third, she's a perfectly charming person."

"And do you like her dancing too?" asked Gabriel in an insolent tone.

"Gabriel, that's enough. I forbid you to mock. You are a child, let's remember, and you are not permitted to judge your aunts."

My mother was always perfect. Was that what made her so distant from us?

Then the summer of 1939 arrived.

Gabriel and I loved summer—having our house filled with friends and cousins, or going out with Papyrus on his motorcycle and sidecar to visit Uncle Geoffroy or Cousin Vincent. They both had children a little older than us but we got along well with them all. Gabriel in particular was fascinated by Michael, the eldest son of Aunt Bette, and did everything to imitate him. I would tease him and get beaten for it. The two of us would repeat our high jinks endlessly—me teasing him, him whacking me—as though we were two out-of-control puppets. Those were our rituals and we never tired of performing them.

We'd had a wonderful summer and the end of August came as a somber knell. Not that we had the least idea about what was really heating up. I was barely ten years old and Gabriel at twelve had a funny voice that would go from soprano to baritone in the same sentence. He also had a few hairs on his chin and now when I teased him, he wouldn't hit me back so much. I understood that we'd come to the end of a certain chapter and it left me somewhat melancholy. There was one day in late August that we spent at the home of Uncle Geoffroy and Aunt Bette, who had organized a big picnic and a game of croquet. Gabriel and Michael had disappeared into some bushes and I hurried in the same direction with my cousin Laure to spy on them. Laure was the daughter of Cousin Vincent and was as bold as I was. I followed her into the little wooded area traversed by a small stream while trying to avoid the stinging nettles. She held branches aside as we walked on, turning toward me as she did so and putting her index finger over her mouth. We heard nothing but the gurgling of the water and the flight of some turtledoves as we walked along wondering where they could be—and then I spotted Michael's back and the profile of my brother, who was passing him a cigarette. Laure looked at me wide-eyed with a mix of admiration and amusement. I told myself that it was good blackmail material to hoard up for a rainy day, and we turned and walked back to the house without them seeing us.

Guests had started returning home. Papyrus, Uncle Geoffroy, and Cousin Vincent were smoking around a table in the garden.

I was going to sit on Papyrus's knees to get a hug, but I hesitated for a moment when I saw how pensive he looked.

"Are you sure of what you're telling me?" he asked Cousin Vincent.

"I spoke with him. They've called up all the aviation reserves."

"And he went?"

"He leaves tomorrow."

"But why are you so surprised, Louis?" exclaimed Uncle Geoffroy. "You're not going to tell us you weren't expecting it?"

"What's going on, Papyrus?" I broke in. "What are you talking about?"

"About a friend, you don't know him."

"And what's happened to him?"

"Nothing, Christiane. Go play with your cousins."

He lowered his knees to encourage me to get off his lap and gave me a gentle tap on the behind.

"Go on, hussar, dismount!"

I never dared disobey any order from Papyrus and so I moved away, though still curious to understand what was happening.

About ten days later, the three of them were called back into military service because France was at war.

Chapter Nineteen

I don't know why I refused to go with my family to Tuscany, but I know it was the right thing to do. Catherine and Lorenzo were reluctant to be together without the protective shield of the family bubble. Luna would be spending little time with them and the prospect of being alone together must have terrified them, but I thought there was no way they were going to use me as a handy substitute for their daughter. Catherine and I were getting along well, but it was most likely because she was afraid to see me go. As for me, I was delighted to be with them in Milan. All traces of friction between me and my son-in-law had been smoothed out, I spent lots of time with Luna, and Catherine was being very agreeable. Lorenzo traveled a lot and my daughter clearly didn't like that. Luna was finishing her thesis and told me often how helpful I'd been. I think she wanted to make me feel good.

"Listen to this!" she called out from a large armchair in the living room where she was slumped with her two legs draped over one side and a book in her hands. "Listen to what he says about technology: 'Sub-Nature must be understood in this, its character of *under* Nature. It will only be so understood if Man rises at least as high in spiritual knowledge of that super-Nature which lies outside the earthly sphere, as he has descended in technical science below it into Sub-Nature.'"

"Oh, that's not a problem I risk having. I can barely answer my cell phone."

"Okay, but Papa, he has been waylaid by Ahriman and the technical civilization."

"He's not the only one. Kids today only know how to play with computers, consoles, and such. I should have paid more attention to poor Aunt Bette. Her Steiner said some interesting things! I was put off by all those esoteric theories, and since I can't believe in anything that's not empirical experience…"

"But Mamie, that's just it. It's in concrete experience that you understand the genius of Steiner! What happened when he died?"

"When he died, Aunt Bette was pregnant and as big as a house. Of course I wasn't born yet. Marie von Sivers was on tour with her eurythmy group and she received a telegram that told her of her husband's declining health and requested she return to Dornach. She let her friend Bette know as soon as possible and rushed to Steiner's sickbed but arrived too late. Bette joined her two days later by train. She says she discovered him dead but radiating peace and serenity. He had worked hard right up to the end and had suffered terribly. I think that those who loved him were relieved to know he had attained that realm between death and rebirth.

"So you believe in that story?"

"What story?"

"That it's the spiritual that renders us human? That in the beginning we proceed directly from the divine and that we've progressively distanced ourselves from it so as to approach the spiritual world in complete liberty? And that the same liberty threatens to see us delivered up completely to Ahriman?"

"Well, I find the materialist imbalance a little dangerous, it's true, but I repeat that for me Steiner's ideas were a continuous wellspring—a little ridiculous and fanatical I would add—for my aunt Bette. In truth, I've only become interested in them recently, thanks to you. I believe I had an overly superficial view of this poor Steiner."

"And yet you just said, 'he attained the realm between death and rebirth.'"

"Oh no, my dear, don't give that any importance! I was only quoting Aunt Bette!"

"Was she sad?"

"No doubt, but I think she didn't have much time to think about it, because, guess what, the evening she arrived in Dornach she gave birth to her son Michael. I always wondered why she gave him that name instead of calling him Rudolf. I never dared ask her why, though, because she probably would have thought that I was teasing her."

"Really? The very same night? That's absolutely incredible!"

"Yes it is. But no matter what I might think or say about her, Aunt Bette was incredible."

"She made you give up your materialist certitudes?" asked Luna, laughing.

"I would never dare venture anything as conclusive as that, but despite all her extravagances she ended up saving my life."

"That's the second time you've said that. Why do you think she saved your life?"

Luna's cell phone rang and she answered excitedly. She then got up to go talk privately in her room. She wanted to be alone with that voice on the other end of the line. It was so nice to be loved, I'll never forget that feeling. I still have tender feelings for all the love I received. It's not nostalgia, it's a form of gratitude for the men I've loved and who loved me back. For the caresses, the expectations, the trembling, the heart pangs, and enormous, crazy joys.

Ah, love, it's beautiful. When I was young I inherited a lot of it as though it were a natural feature, like my green eyes or my fragile fingernails, and I still remember how surprised I was when I discovered that it had slipped through my fingers like warm water. I don't at all regret what replaced it—affection, another way of being alone, also peace. And in this new setup there was really only room for you, my husband, you alone could survive all this calm abdication. After all this dusty tumult and sighing had gone out the window and I turned toward the obscurity of our bedroom, I saw you: solid and silent but so present, and you gave me your hand. What remains of all the upheaval? We do. We're all that remains.

Even after your death, we're still all that remains.

"Do you know why your aunt Bette named her son Michael?"

Luna had returned and was trying to pick up the conversation where we'd left off.

"No, it's odd, isn't it?"

"Not at all. For Rudolf Steiner, man, once he had attained his autonomy, needs a guide to reunite with the divine. Just as Jesus Christ took bodily form to save us from the evil influence of Ahriman, the archangel Michael's mission, according to him, was to help us get closer to the world of spirit. That's why Aunt Bette named her son Michael."

"But her son was hardly an archangel, all he did was get into trouble, with Gabriel right on his heels most of the time."

"The two archangels had taken human form."

"You can say that again, more human than those two doesn't exist!"

"And Cousin Vincent? Did he name his son Raphael?"

"No, he didn't. He named him Victor."

"I'm going out to dinner tonight."

"Is he good-looking?"

"Yes."

"Intelligent?"

"Yes."

Since we'd be alone that evening, I suggested to Catherine that she choose a restaurant she liked and I'd treat for dinner. As we walked in front of the museum, we passed a violinist who was playing Schubert. Catherine was about to walk by without the least glance in the direction of the musician.

"What are you doing?" I asked her with surprise.

"What do you mean what am I doing? I'm walking to the restaurant. We have to go up via Solferino."

"So don't you give musicians money anymore?"

"When I feel like it I do."

"Ah."

I bent down to place a coin in his open case. I had always taught Catherine to give money to musicians. I consider it the least we can do given all the beauty they bring to the street, and since she was very young Catherine always did. Watch out, Christiane, you old biddy, and don't cover with some political argument your old mother octopus reflexes. But I can't resist: "Well, I always feel like it."

Catherine shrugged her shoulders as though to say that was my problem.

The restaurant where we had reserved a table for two was run by a charming gentleman—a man who seemed to come straight from the sort of book I love, books filled with strong-willed characters and heroes who don't age. He was very elegant with round red eyeglass frames and a magnificent mustache that gave him an air of Colonel Chabert or Count Vronsky. He wore Scottish plaid trousers and two-toned shoes—I found him simply stunning. Besides that, he spoke to me in excellent French. I don't have much of an appetite anymore except for seafood, but the meal was delicious. I don't know if it was the Dolcetto d'Alba or being alone with my daughter, but I really enjoyed my evening.

"You know, Catherine, I was very pleased with you in the car yesterday."

"Oh really, why?"

She looked at me while holding a fork full of zucchini stuffed with ricotta near her mouth and waited for my answer.

"That seems to surprise you."

"Yes, it does."

"Why?"

"Because most of the time I don't please you very much."

"Oh, why do you say that?"

"Because you criticize me all the time."

"You're the one who criticizes me all the time," I replied a little too emphatically.

"I criticize you because you criticize me."

"Oh Catherine, are you serious?"

"Are you saying you don't realize it? 'Catherine, you're too serious,' 'Catherine, you're too boring,' 'Catherine, you have no imagination, no seductive side, no devilishness,' and on and on."

"Oh my poor dear, it's terrible to think that. You're severe too: 'Mother, you're a windbag,' 'Mother, why are you still smoking at your age?' 'Mother, you can't do anything right.' Sometimes I get the feeling *you* are trying to raise *me*."

"It's true I find your constant search for some new angle irritating."

"What do you mean, my search for a new angle?"

"It's like you're constantly trying to be original and I find it irritating. It's true, Mother, why can't you just do the normal thing once in a while?"

"And you, why can't you ever get off the beaten path?"

"Because you're my mother and I've had my fill of walks through the jungle. I've always dreamed of a humble cottage and garden. I always needed a well-marked, orderly space, but you always found that boring. So how did I please you driving yesterday?"

"I don't dare say anymore."

"Okay, got it. Do you see how predictable you are behind your grand originality?"

"You're mean."

"Right, get it out there! So I pleased you when I yelled at the car that cut me off and lowered my window to insult the guy."

I stared humbly at my plate. That was in fact what had pleased me so much. She said everything in Italian and I didn't understand a word, but it came out of her like a geyser and I was really pleased to see her let loose for once.

"You see, I know you pretty well, don't I?" After an awkward moment of silence, she continued: "So you see, I resemble your mother. I like routines, muted colors, and clichés."

"My mother would never have insulted the driver the way you did yesterday."

"Well, I have a little bit of you, a tiny little bit, just a few drops."

I pretended that I needed to go to the ladies' room. In fact I was overcome with the most horrible desire to cry. I hated myself. Just at the moment when my dear daughter was finally confronting the problem she had with me, the big crumbling and stumbling baby that I was collapsed into a sullen puddle. I closed the toilet seat, sat down, and started plugging my tear ducts.

When I returned to the table she was speaking with the restaurant owner.

"Mother, Italo says you're magnificent."

"It's true, you are superb!" He rolled his *r*'s in a charming way.

"You are very kind, but really I don't think I am. I wasn't bad-looking when I was young, a very long time ago."

"But this exaggerated emphasis on youth is unbearable. It's gone in the blink of an eye and people spend the rest of their long lives thinking only of that short season."

"It's true," I said, amused. "But it's especially you men who adore youth. We women, I think we'd be more comfortable with the passage of time if we weren't terrified of losing you."

"I'm not like that. On the contrary, the young get on my nerves."

"Really? The young make me gentler. And you, Catherine?"

"They intrigue me. I was never young."

The restaurant owner left to attend to other guests and we remained silent for a moment.

"I'm sorry to have caused you pain," said Catherine, holding out her hand.

"Don't feel sorry. It's good to speak openly with each other."

"I want you to know that despite everything I love you very much."

"Of course, I know that. I have no resentment, I assure you. And perhaps you're right that I'm judgmental without realizing it. In any case I'm enormously pleased with you, Catherine."

"No, you love me a lot, but I don't please you. It's people like your new friend Josephine who please you."

"Why do you bring her up? Josephine pleases me a lot, but you're my daughter."

"If we had crossed paths at university, you would never have wanted to get to know me."

"Well there you're totally mistaken! I would certainly have become your best friend."

"So your Josephine, it's just an act then? Just because you think it's cool to be friends with a young, poor black woman?"

"A generous, intelligent, funny, and courageous black woman."

"Is that true?"

"Yes, very true. If you knew Josephine better, you would be fond of her too — and if you knew me better, you'd know that I don't want to change anything about you."

"Shall we go home?"

"Yes, of course."

I paid the bill, we said a warm goodbye to the original and clever owner, and then we stepped out into the hot night air.

When we passed by the violinist again, Catherine placed a five-euro bill into his case. I pretended not to have noticed.

Chapter Twenty

I've only kept fragmentary memories of the war, pieces that don't fit together, like an abandoned picture puzzle. I remember my mother's cousin Géraud, a good-for-nothing who was too young to fight but helped us out some. I remember how it seemed there were only women because all the men had gone off to fight. I also remember kind Jeanne who tried to get us to like Jerusalem artichokes. I also remember my mother being surprisingly active and courageous. She spent a lot of time praying, but she also worked long hours in the vegetable garden behind the stables, sewing clothes to give away, even house cleaning when there was no one else to do it. I don't know about Gabriel, but for me these memories are mostly warm and pleasant. I was about twelve then and was perfectly capable of donning a serious look when the war was under discussion, but I didn't have the faintest idea about fear tying one's stomach in knots or the anxiety of death and defeat.

It was precisely in the bull's-eye of my juvenile confidence in existence that fate struck its fatal blow, the event that breaks forever the balance of one's life, transporting the person from the morning's sweetness to night's biting cold.

We were at the table when out the window we saw Aunt Bette's car coming down the allée.

"When I'm older I'll drive like Aunt Bette," I said as I ate my soup.

"I'm not sure that's proper for a woman."

"Why not? You don't have to wear a bathing suit to drive!" Gabriel quipped.

"Don't be insolent, Gabriel! You know that's not what I meant. Just imagine if she had a mechanical problem and found herself alone in the middle of nowhere. She'd be prey to who knows what scoundrel."

"But what if you sprain your ankle on the way back from church? It's the same thing!"

Incensed, Mother was about to come back with another remark of her own when Aunt Bette, looking pale and trembling, walked in.

"Marguerite, can you come with me right away?"

"Where?"

"Follow me."

Mother followed her. Gabriel and I ran immediately to one of the large windowpanes to spy on them and try to understand what it might be about. We saw Aunt Bette speaking with our mother, who then put her head in her hands, and Aunt Bette hugged her. They then walked to the car, got in and drove off.

"What's happening?"

"I don't know but it looks serious," Gabriel answered somberly.

"Papyrus?" I asked trembling.

"Of course not! She would have told us, we're his children, aren't we?"

"It's true," I said heaving a big sigh.

"I bet it's Uncle Geoffroy, you know."

"Poor man! But I'd rather it be him than Papyrus!"

"Sure, but he is awfully nice, Uncle Geoffroy."

"That's true. How do you think it happened?" I asked Gabriel.

"He must have got a bullet in the head."

"Poor man. That must have hurt like hell."

"You got that right."

Jeanne appeared and not seeing our mother asked what was going on.

"Uncle Geoffroy is dead," I blurted out to prevent Gabriel from having the pleasure of announcing bad news.

"How awful!" said Jeanne. "How did that happen?"

"He most likely got shot in the head," said Gabriel.

"How awful! My little dears, what are we going to do to get your minds on something else? It's horrible. Your uncle Geoffroy was so nice!"

I burst into tears. Honestly though, I think amid all our dramatic efforts to conjure away the possibility of losing Papyrus, there was also true sadness at the thought of losing Uncle Geoffroy. The fact is that Uncle Geoffroy would return from the front without a scratch, whereas Papyrus got a piece of shrapnel lodged in his side, but it luckily missed his spinal cord. An ambulance took him to a military hospital. He was in critical condition and an operation was performed, though they could not extract the shard from his spine. He was lucky that it hit him from the side, otherwise he would have surely died or been paralyzed.

When Aunt Bette learned the news from her husband, who had been notified by telegram, Papyrus had already been transported to the hospital in Amiens. There he continued to be in terrible pain even though he'd been given frequent injections of morphine. My mother spent several weeks traveling between Amiens, where her mother, our grandma Éléonore, lived, and Warvillers, where my brother and I stayed. Then came the truce and the Germans invaded the region. Because we were in the occupied zone, my mother had to obtain a pass to go to Amiens. She received it with no trouble, probably because Aunt Bette, who spoke fluent German, accompanied her and was therefore able to help with formulating the request.

I remember the snow that covered the Somme, the cold mornings that emerged slowly from the night, and Gabriel and me walking to school seeing our breath and hearing our steps crunch on the frosty ground as we walked in silence hurrying for once to get to school because it was a warm refuge. I remember our too heavy school satchels and our gloves and socks that were made of a coarse, itchy wool. I remember the smell of warm bread when we passed in front of the bakery and how it made our mouths water. I remember the sweet waiting period before Christmas. We knew there would be no presents, but the magic of Christmas is nevertheless indestructible in the hearts of children. I remember the crèche in a corner of the classroom and the paper stars that we painted and hung up to decorate the blackboard and Madame Valence's desk. I also remember Pascale Dagnan, who brought a box of candy that she joyfully distributed to everyone in the class. I remember my own feeling of joy mixed with gray shades of melancholy—my first experience of a way of being happy when a feeling of safety would follow a consciousness of having escaped some danger. For example, when in my hot living room I watch the thunderstorm erupt over Saint-Sulpice. I also remember the mass when we would loudly sing *Cantate Domino*.

I remember well the end of a school day with little light left in the sky and all sorts of cars parked out front. There was a small white truck and the cars of Aunt Bette and Cousin Vincent. We ran as fast as we could and discovered a whole group of people in our living room.

"Ah, here are the children," said Uncle Geoffroy with open welcoming arms. "It's a happy day for us all: your father has come back home!"

"No, no, come back this instant!" our mother cried just as we were running up the stairs to go and hug Papyrus.

"Why?" asked Gabriel.

"Because he's exhausted and you have to be very gentle with him," answered Uncle Geoffroy in a grave manner.

We came back down. We were told that Papyrus was in very bad shape and that he would need months to recover and that we were to be kind and patient. All of that formed a big knot of nerves in our stomachs and Aunt Bette sensed this.

"Maybe the children could go and hug their father for just a brief moment. I think it would be reassuring for them. What do you think, Doctor Morel?"

"Yes, of course. The important thing, children, is not to tire him, do you understand? So you may go give him a kiss, but then you must leave him."

We climbed the stairs behind Mother and Uncle Geoffroy. My heart was beating fast and I think Gabriel's was too, even though lately he had been starting to imitate the men and play the stiff tough guy.

Our mother gently opened the door. It creaked a bit and she slipped into Papyrus's room alone. We heard her ask him if he'd like to kiss the children and his mumbled baritone *Oui* in reply. She returned and motioned for us to enter. We had not seen our father for many months and this reunion was a terrible shock. He was lying in his bed seemingly with no energy whatsoever. His worn skin hung on his bones like an old yellow rag, his light-colored eyes, usually so impishly twinkling, seemed to be hiding like two frightened kittens, and his bony hands gripped the covers of the bed in a desperate gesture of hanging on for dear life.

I approached, terrified by this phantom of the person whom I had loved so much, but lacking the courage to bend and kiss him. I saw on Gabriel's face a look of devastation that he tried to hide behind a forced smile.

"Gosh, Papyrus, they certainly roughed you up bad, those goddamn Krauts!"

Papyrus looked disoriented for a few seconds and then gave out a weak laugh.

"You said it!" he whispered feebly.

He then looked at me and made a gesture with his bony hand for me to come closer. I did, my heart still pounding, and when I leaned over to put my lips on his forehead, I was in tears. My mother tore me immediately from my father's arms and apologized to him: "It's the emotion, she missed you so much! All right, children, that's enough for today, your father is fatigued from his journey. Say good night and be off."

When we were out of the room Gabriel chewed me out.

"Really, Christiane, it wasn't so great of you to start crying in his arms!"

"Stop it, Gabriel, stop it! It hurts enough already without you piling on too."

I ran to my room sobbing. My brother followed me and for the second time in his life was unbelievably kind. He patted my hair in silence and let me cry out everything I had inside without interrupting me.

Papyrus would never die as much as he died that day. When we put him in the ground years later, I only resumed the grieving that had overwhelmed me the day of his return.

After that there was Christmas Eve and our walk through the black night to the midnight mass. Then the festivities back at the house with uncles and cousins and Aunt Bette, who was very elegant as always, and Mother taciturn and solemn as always. I remember the next morning when despite the circumstances a few presents were there to surprise us under the decorated Christmas tree, and Papyrus, leaning stiffly and painfully on two canes, made it out of his room for the first time.

The winter passed, cold and windy—the cries of menacing crows and the north wind were a fitting accompaniment to our misfortunes. Jeanne the cook never tired of trying to jolly us into better spirits — repeating that we were "*pauvres choux*" until we ended up believing it ourselves. And over time without us noticing we grew up. I was no longer bored, Gabriel disappeared for longer periods of time, and Mother continued her sad life between church and embroidery. We didn't go often to the homes of Uncle Geoffroy or Cousin Vincent because our mother refused to leave Papyrus alone.

As the weather improved so did Papyrus. He got up more often and gained some weight. Little by little his irregular good features returned and he no longer had that terrified look. Nevertheless it was clear that the joie de vivre that he'd struggled hard to rebuild after the first war was gone for good after the second. He spent a lot of time in his room and less time on horseback. He was also less affectionate and more short-tempered. The sidecar was never brought out of the garage anymore and I didn't dare ask to be taken on a ride.

Gabriel was almost a grown man — during the occupation one grew up fast. We didn't have much to eat and felt constantly under threat. He attended a lycée in Amiens and lived with our grandma Éléonore. On Saturday at noon Mother and I would watch for his return, looking out the big windows in the living room until we saw him.

Papyrus was less interested in us then. He always had a vacant look, except when with his brother and cousin he'd start talking about politics and criticizing Marshal Pétain, the hero they had so loved in 1918 who then betrayed them. Uncle Geoffroy spoke a lot about a certain de Gaulle and how he wanted to join him in England. The women spoke hardly at all. Gabriel and his cousin Michael, on the other hand, paid close attention to all that was said.

The few times that I went into Papyrus's room, I noticed there was always a gray tube with a syringe on his bedside table. I asked him what that was and he replied, "It's morphine. It's to take away the pain."

"Because you're still in a lot of pain?"

"No, thanks to the morphine it's not so bad."

But when one day at the table I had a terrible headache and said it would need a little morphine, my mother looked directly at me with a concerned and frightened look.

"Who spoke to you about morphine?"

"Papyrus."

"Your father takes that for his health, but don't go around repeating that to everyone, it could be misinterpreted."

"Why, if it helps him have less pain?"

"Still."

I later overheard Mother arguing with Uncle Geoffroy about it all:

"I spoke about it with Dr. Morel, who says there is no longer any reason to continue with that dirty stuff."

"Fine, then have it taken away from him!"

"He won't hear of it. I've tried everything but he gets absolutely furious whenever the subject is brought up."

"And Dr. Morel, has he tried talking to him about it?"

"Of course! He's been telling me for months that he's concerned by it and that we need to begin weaning him off it."

"Well, if he's not open to reason, we'll have to use force."

"What are you talking about?" I asked with an innocent air, even though I knew perfectly well what *it* was that they were talking about.

"These matters are no concern of yours, Christiane, so let the adults talk by themselves."

In early May when the wind no longer whipped its way across the plain, we could sit outside in the garden and enjoy the first rays of sun. My region is infinitely flat, as the great Jacques Brel put it so well, and with only a few groves of oak and beech trees to block its right of way, the north wind in springtime was often a nuisance.

We were sitting in the garden—Gabriel and I and Aunt Bette and Mother—while Uncle Geoffroy, a nurse, and Dr. Morel tried to calm down Papyrus, who was screaming. We were all silent and eager for it to end. Papyrus had been so violent that they had placed him in a straitjacket, but we did not see that happen. Gabriel's mourning for our father had transformed into intense hostility toward him. I was simply sad, terribly sad, as though I had witnessed an angel fall from the sky. And this fall was rather spectacular! Amid an explosion of breaking glass and the cries of our uncle and the doctor, we saw catapulted before our astonished eyes a white package tied up like a leg of lamb: my father.

Everyone rushed to stand around the form that was writhing on the ground and moaning. The women were in tears and the men looked on with pale stares. Papyrus complained of being in terrible pain. He'd broken his leg in the struggle.

While everyone was busying themselves with getting him back to his room, and Dr. Morel returned to his office to get what he needed to make a cast, Aunt Bette took us aside to explain our father's problem, how he'd become addicted to his medicine, and how difficult it was to overcome that addiction.

"That's all he needed," said Gabriel.

"It's true, poor man, he's really been through the wringer."

"For Chrissake, addicted to his medicine! He could have spared us that!"

"But it's not his fault, Gabriel! His wounds were terrible and he probably wouldn't have survived the pain without morphine. The problem is that he took it for a long time and he can't go without it."

"Even if he really tries?"

"Gabriel, quit being so hard on him, you don't know what you're talking about!" said Aunt Bette, whose cheeks were red with anger. "Do you know what he's gone through? Your father is a hero, don't judge him like that!"

"And yet despite all these heroes, we've got Krauts overrunning the whole country!"

Gabriel stood up to go. His anger and insolence left Aunt Bette and me speechless.

Chapter Twenty-One

I never spied on my husband, even during my worst fits of jealousy. I would like to be able to claim some form of coherence when it comes to the defense of my private life and by extension that of others, but the truth is rather different. I've always been terribly afraid of what lay hidden under masks, of the horrible things in the dark shadows. For me secrets have always been sealed in the stink of our ignoble episodes, and I think those who reveal them are doing something akin to eating dung.

One such episode happened in the summer of 1943.

I was fourteen years old and had started to be invited to a few balls that took place in the region. Gabriel, who was two years older, and my cousins always accompanied me. I rather enjoyed flirting with boys and gossiping with my cousin Laure. Michael could drive and we'd often pile into his convertible and ride with our hair in the wind on starry nights. Youth is a sort of living faith, and nothing, not even war, can clip its wings. Gabriel had taken on his father's taste for ladies and the good life, and I would not be surprised if he lost his virginity during that summer vacation. During these balls, he'd always disappear with the prettiest girl there and later emerge from some clump of bushes with a knowing, satisfied look. People always considered me funny, and I sold my soul to make those around me laugh. Sometimes I went a little too far with my sharp tongue — earning the admiration of the young and the mistrust of the adults.

Papyrus had recovered from his accident. He got stronger, began riding more again, and seemed to have overcome his morphine problem. But he remained distant and reserved. He was casually kind to us without really picking up on Gabriel's hostility or my melancholy over finding him so inaccessible. My mother also walled herself behind a brusque austerity and except for the village priest she would see no one unless she had to.

Since the Germans seized everything that our wheat fields and cattle farms produced, we were certainly not living comfortably, but at the same time we couldn't complain, given the real hardship endured by most of our fellow citizens. Papyrus did not take an active interest in the affairs of the farm and left his assistant Monsieur Carbon to manage things in his place. Aunt Bette came to see us almost every day and took long rides on horseback with Papyrus.

One day she came back alone and visibly agitated. When I asked her what had happened to Papyrus, she replied curtly that he would be coming back soon. She then gave me a quick peck on the forehead, got in her car, and drove off in a hurry. Papyrus saw her from far off leaving along the allée. He nudged his horse with his heels and made off in her direction, crying, "Bette, Bette, wait!" But she paid no attention, and even though he accelerated into a

quick gallop and jumped the rock wall and hedge that separated the château's grounds from the allée, he was not able
to catch up with her. I watched all of this in total astonish-
ment. What could he have done to Bette that would make
the two of them behave this way? He rode his horse back
to the stable. Seeing his somber face, the stableman asked
him if everything was all right. "Of course everything's all
right," he snapped back with such rage in his voice that it
was clear that everything was all wrong.

When my cousins and brother returned from playing
tennis, Papyrus had already gone up to his room. I would
have liked to tell Gabriel what I had seen, but there was
no way to say it to him away from the others. We decided
to have a game of croquet. While some were placing the
wickets, others went to get the balls and mallets. I went off
to the kitchen to prepare a tray with glasses and lemon selt-
zer. I entered the pantry to look for a lemon—Mother was
frugal with them and had taught me how to use even the
rind. The pantry was a little room behind the kitchen. As
I approached I heard the moaning of a woman. I of course
had no idea about lovemaking, but I was instantly aware
that I had invaded some private intimate moment. Instead
of withdrawing, however, I stepped quietly closer and ris-
ing on my tiptoes I looked through the window at the top
of the door and saw what was going on inside. Jeanne was
leaning with clenched hands against a buffet, her skirts
gathered up above her waist, and the hands of a man held
her naked breasts. The trousers of the man holding her
were down below his knees and his face was buried in the
back of her neck. I knew right away that it was Papyrus. I

fell to the ground feeling very dizzy. A feeling of disgust made me nearly vomit.

I then hightailed it out of there and ran toward the fields until I was out of breath. When I stopped, panting and upset, I threw myself on the ground and spread out my arms. Above me white clouds danced in the blue sky and I felt the odd consoling power of being cared for by the beauty of the infinite.

Gabriel was obsessed by the occupation and couldn't talk about anything else. He spent all his free time with his cousin Michael elaborating plans to make life difficult for the Krauts. After much waiting, an opportunity presented itself. Michael came over one Saturday in October and the two of them went off to sit in my oak tree. I hated feeling excluded, and what's more, that tree belonged to Gabriel and me—especially to me, because it had been hollowed out for my baptism. So I followed them.

"What do you have to say to each other that no one else can hear?"

"Leave us alone, Christiane, this is men's stuff."

"But why?" said Michael. "She can be useful to us. Don't you trust your sister?"

"It has nothing to do with trust. Of course I trust her, it's just that I don't want something to happen to her."

"She's entitled to fight against the Heinies like the rest of us! Besides, Christiane's no wimp!"

"Okay, fine, stay with us then, but keep your mouth shut."

"Of course I will," I said, delighted to be included in their circle and to have been complimented by the cousin we both so admired.

"Do you know what the FTP is?" Michael asked us in a lower voice.

"Of course," replied Gabriel, disdainfully shrugging his shoulders.

"And you Christiane?"

"Uh, sort of." I was embarrassed to admit my ignorance.

"She has no idea what it is," Gabriel interjected. "It's the Francs-Tireurs et Partisans movement, a clandestine resistance organization."

"Oh right, and so what about them?"

"Well, the baker is one of them," said Michael. "And because he knows what I think, he approached me at mass last Sunday and asked me to help him get two escaped prisoners across the Somme. It has to be done quickly because the people hiding them are starting to get nervous about being caught."

"But every bridge is blocked by Germans. Without an *Ausweis* they can never cross!"

"I know that, but we can help them."

"How?"

"You know the textile factory not far from my house?"

"You mean the big gray building just off the main road?"

"That's the one. I know the concierge, who also thinks as we do."

"So?"

"Behind the factory there's a stream that crosses the factory's property and empties into the Somme. There's a little bridge between its two banks. The concierge will let us onto the grounds and it will be easy to get them through the prohibited zone. I volunteered to do it, but I prefer to have someone along as lookout and I thought of you."

"I'm in. Are you kidding, I've been waiting for a chance like this!"

"Me too, I'm in!"

"Christiane, for this first time it's better that you don't come, but I take very seriously your offer to help. Let us go ahead with this, and the next time there's something to do, you'll be a part of it."

"Do your parents know about this?"

"No, but I'm sure they'd approve."

"Even your mother?"

"Are you asking that because she's Swiss and an admirer of an Austrian?"

"Maybe."

"But the Austrian in question hated Nazism, and the Swiss, even if they're officially neutral, aren't fond of the Nazis either," Michael answered laughing. Then he gave Gabriel's shoulder a condescending affectionate tap.

It's true that we were an ignorant bunch of hicks!

The operation was set to take place the following Saturday. The factory's workers would be gone and the two cousins would only have to deal with the concierge, their accomplice. They went off by car that morning. I was getting ready for a day of worrying until their return. If Papyrus had still been Papyrus, I would have shared my waiting and worrying with him, but since the day I came upon him with Jeanne, I did everything I could to avoid him. He sometimes tried to approach me, but I politely detested this impostor who had taken over the body of the father I so loved.

I tried to kill time with books and walks, but I couldn't think of anything besides what Gabriel and Michael must be up to.

I heard loud voices coming from above and went to the stairs to hear what was going on. The noise was very surprising to me because usually all adult conflicts, resentments, and jealousies were communicated in near silence, from one hostile bile duct to another. For them anger was yellow—I never would have said that my mother was red with anger. About Papyrus, I would have said he was green with anger. But the red-hot, bloody anger of people who love each other, only Gabriel and I knew what that was. And yet suddenly, there on the floor above, a fire of anger had erupted with all the variations that flames have: red for consummated love, yellow for bitterness, and green for hatred and resentment.

"You promised me you weren't going to use any anymore! You tricked me, you've tricked all of us!"

"Marguerite, quit tyrannizing me! Can't you see I'm suffocating? I've had it with you, with this prison, this dull gray life. I can't take any more of you and your perfection and all the hypocrisy that goes with it!"

"What hypocrisy are you talking about? I've done nothing but love you all my life!"

"What do you know about love? You've known nothing else and you're so moralizing you'd never admit otherwise anyway."

"Louis, you are being deeply hurtful! What did I ever do to you? I've spent my whole life loving you and trying to make you happy! It's not my fault if I don't have Bette's charms or the freshness of a young woman."

"Bette has nothing to do it."

"But she's the one who discovered you're still taking that poison."

"I made the mistake of confiding in her when we were out riding."

"She waited several months before telling me about it, but now you have to stop! I'm begging you to stop!"

"I'm nearly fifty and I don't want to die of suffocation in this drab life we're living."

"Louis, what are you going to do?"

The voices were getting closer and suddenly I heard the footsteps of my father followed by my mother descending the stairs — I stood there stoically and waited. Papyrus was wearing a cape and black helmet and putting on gloves. My mother followed behind imploring him:

"Where are you going? Are you forgetting you have a piece of metal lodged in your spine?"

He stopped in front of me, turned toward her, and with a steely hardness that I never would have thought possible from him, lashed out: "That's enough, Marguerite! Enough! Goodbye."

Mother collapsed at the foot of the stairs crying. Papyrus was facing me. Suddenly that face took on all the sweetness of long ago and the sight brought tears to my eyes.

"Pardon me, my Christiane, I ask the three of you to pardon me, but I can't go on anymore."

He went out the door and I did nothing to stop him. A few minutes later I heard the engine noise of his motorcycle and sidecar going off down the allée. It took a few minutes for the noise to fade, only to be replaced by the leaden silence of abandonment.

When my brother got back all excited from his adventure, he found Mother still slumped at the bottom step of the stairs. He shot me an inquiring look and I explained the situation. He then clenched his fists and jaw and said, "Mother, we'll be just as well without that bastard."

"Gabriel, I forbid you to speak of your father that way!"

Papyrus never returned to the château.

Chapter Twenty-Two

S o according to your Steiner, we alone are responsible for what happens to us?" Josephine asked while leaning in as though to confide in me.

"Insofar as we choose beforehand to live all that we live, yes."

"And do you believe that?"

"No, and he's not *my* Steiner, although I do believe that to a large extent we are capable of directing our existence."

"I have trouble believing that the people who live the dramatic events that are reported in the news every day have chosen those destinies before they arrive on the planet!"

"And yet that's what Steiner would say."

"There's a sort of megalomaniac side to his way of thinking. But on second thought, that might be the only aspect of all this that pleases me, the idea that I'm not the victim of anything, that I've decided everything."

She took a sip of her green tea and stared out into space.

"So chance doesn't exist?"

"According to him, no it doesn't."

"So if the two of us met, it's because we decided to on some level? What if I had wanted to meet you, but you didn't, or the reverse? What's he say about that, your Steiner?"

"Oh, Josephine, you're wearing me out! Ask Luna. Really I don't know that much about him. Can we change the subject? I really would like to talk to you about something else."

"Go right ahead."

"Okay, but I don't know how to say this without putting you in an embarrassing situation."

"Don't worry, Christiane, I can defend myself, you know."

"Against adversity, certainly, but maybe not against friendship."

"And why should I have to defend myself against friendship?"

"Because I'm alone and old and intrusive."

"You're no longer that young, but otherwise I don't agree with you. You're neither alone nor intrusive. What do you want to ask me?"

"What are you doing this summer?"

"I'm on vacation until mid-August and then I'm working."

"And do you have any plans?"

"What could I have for plans? Maybe a few days with Mita, but not long, we can't really afford much."

"I'd like to spend a few days in Brittany with you."

"With me?"

"Yes."

"My dear Christiane, I don't have the money for that."

"But I do."

"But you're you."

"It would be my treat, of course."

"No, that's not possible!"

"Why not?"

"I don't like being in debt to others, not even to people I like."

"You'd be depriving me of a lot of happiness for nothing, Josephine."

"It's not nothing. Do you know what it means to be linked by indebtedness to someone? It would disfigure everything between us. I wouldn't be my natural self, instead I'd be constantly thinking about how I'm taking a fancy vacation thanks to you; and you, you'd soon be treating me as your lady in waiting."

"Josephine, what if we prove to each other that we're better than those clichés?"

"But no one's better than them, Christiane! To me, you're a true friend. I don't want to risk messing everything up for the sake of a week at the seaside, do you understand?"

"It's crazy though to deprive ourselves of a wonderful moment together on account of money problems that don't even exist."

"They don't exist for you, Christiane, and so lucky you, but for me it's a very different matter."

"I don't want that to be the case."

"Well, you'll have to ask your Steiner to ship you off to another planet. Here money decides everything—everything except friendship."

"So shall I stay in Paris with you?"

"Yes, and I'll invite you out to dinner at an African restaurant in the rue Lepic."

"And I'll invite you to the theater one evening."

"Deal!"

"That is unless the sound of the sea…the gulls…eating oysters at sunset…"

"It's not nice what you're doing, you know."

"But it would be so simple if you would just be a little more trusting, Josephine."

"No, Christiane. No means no."

Luckily things worked out all on their own because I needed a car to get to Saint-Briac in early August and Josephine volunteered to drive me there. That's how, little by little, I managed to lure her to Brittany. One of her friends loaned her an old Renault. With some effort I let her pay for the gas and some provisions without saying a word. Josephine was the kindest and most cheerful person imaginable, but she knew how to command respect and so I behaved myself.

"I thank you for existing, Josephine. Without you I would be alone and more susceptible to bouts of melancholy. You see, this beach is so nice in the evening around seven, but really unbearable during the day. When Catherine was little it was different. We would always set up here, right where we are now, but there wasn't this crowd of people all around. I don't know where they've all come from these past few years."

"Is your daughter doing better?"

"I hope so. It really breaks my heart to see her suffer."

"Maybe you should have stayed there with her."

"Certainly not."

"Do you miss her?"

"Yes."

"Myself, I don't think I regret not having children."

"But you still can."

"Technically speaking yes, but it's still awfully late. I'm forty-three. Plus, I'm not interested in finding a mate."

"No one? As beautiful as you are?"

"That has nothing to do with it!"

"What about uncomplicated dating or adventures?"

"What do you mean by that?"

"Oh don't play the innocent! You know very well what I mean!"

"Frankly, that doesn't interest me at all at the moment. And you?"

"We can stop there. I dislike this sort of discussion."

"But Christiane, you're the one who started it!"

"Yes, but let's stop anyway, okay?"

"Oh, so when it's about you we can 'stop there,' but if it's about my private life it's okay for you to know everything?"

"I'm old. It's terrible an old woman talking about love."

"Really, old girl, sometimes you say the stupidest things."

A silence followed. Josephine got up to go in the water. I watched her come back, her sculpted ebony body, the sparkling ocean water dripping off her under the red late afternoon sun. I asked her how she managed being on her own.

"Do you mean having no family?"

"Yes, but not just that."

"I lost my love, Christiane. And you, how do you do it? You seem to manage pretty well too. We simply have no other choice."

"True, but I always have the feeling that a piece of me is floating somewhere else in the universe, or in some other time. I never manage to be *here*, *now*."

"With me it's more like a hole in my stomach. I can get nourishment from everything I encounter, but still there's this hole here." She pointed to a spot at the level of her sternum. "But we should keep in mind that despite all, we've triumphed."

"Over what?"

"Over the general ugliness. Human dramas have not succeeded in crushing us. Were you loved?"

"Yes, by men and by my brother maybe. By my parents, I don't know."

"Oh, your Papyrus, he adored you before he started taking drugs!"

"Yes, that's true."

"And your mother, a saint like that, of course she loved you."

"I don't know."

"Well, in any case, I like you a lot."

"I know, and I feel the same about you. In fact, we could say that at this point in our lives when we miss everything that we really don't lack for anything."

"Oh yes, there *is* something that we cruelly lack!"

"Please, don't say anything sad!"

"No, it's a lack that we can easily remedy!"

"What?"

"A large plate of shellfish and a cold bottle of dry white wine!"

Yes, Josephine had that admirable character trait—she adored seafood.

Luna and Josephine offered me the feeling of intimate closeness that old people generally have to do without. The swallowing up of our worlds calls forth the specter of death, but some invincible resistance comes with their presence. Maybe it's because they love making me talk about my past. What began as Luna's intellectual interest in Rudolf Steiner gradually became a sort of archeological exploration of her roots. Was she hoping her ancestors would unlock the great mystery of her existence? Was she looking to find some map or key to her fate through my life story? When she asked for the third time, "Why do you say Bette saved your life?" was she looking for the origin of her own life?

Whatever the case may be, here's how Bette saved my life.

Chapter Twenty-Three

A t the end of the war I was already going to high school and living with my grandmother Éléonore—a severe, gruff woman who reprimanded us constantly. Gabriel wanted to attend Saint-Cyr and was becoming quite a good student. My dream, after graduating from high school, was to go to university to study philosophy—but my mother and grandmother considered that not at all proper. Completing high school and obtaining my baccalaureate was already for me a major triumph, since both of them had done all they could to divert me toward embroidery and similar activities at a horrendous school that trained girls to become perfect little homemakers. Their insistence was directly proportional to their displeasure with my behavior, which for them lacked femininity. Despite what they believed, however, I had a lot of success among the boys of my age.

Aunt Bette was very useful in these negotiations, even though Grandma Éléonore felt complete contempt for her.

"That Bette," she'd say, her mouth full of disgust, "does not inspire the least confidence. A total Jezebel—or Salomé! I've heard she did obscene dances covered in veils!

To think that she managed to marry my Enguerrand and that imbecile Geoffroy to boot!"

My mother, on the other hand, maintained a certain admiration mixed with jealousy for her, and so when Bette praised the advantages of culture and education for a young woman who could no longer count on the material support of a father, she kept her mouth shut. Bette's argument was strengthened by the undeniably impoverished state of things at the château. Mother did not know how to manage the farmhands who worked the land and many of the young men wanted to leave and work in cities. She was therefore forced to let Jeanne go along with the other servants, and eventually ended up living at her mother's place too. The château fell into a sad decline.

For my mother and grandmother, sudden humiliation gradually replaced the pain of loss. My mother had been sincerely in love with my father—that's something I've never doubted for a second. The people we socialized with, *notre milieu*, as my mother called them, formed an impregnable wall between us and the rest of the world. But that same milieu was unable to pardon a family scandal like ours. In truth, they spoke of nothing else, and they should have been grateful to us for finally shaking up the comforter that lay over the flat surface of their lives, but that would not have been compatible with the true benefit that our family drama offered them. The saga gave them endless opportunities to feel superior and point accusing, judging index fingers at us. There were a few generous souls among them who managed to sigh, "Ah, the poor children!"—but it only took the slightest gaffe or misstep, usually on Gabriel's part, for the entire clique to declare scornfully, "He's just like his father!" For them, in other words, shame was genetically transmitted and therefore we were in a way guilty from birth because we were the off-spring of a scoundrel.

I had a few friends, but I sensed that I was being treated with aloof curiosity and that irritated me. The only people I really got along with still were my cousins, and so Gabriel and I would spend time at their houses whenever we had the chance.

Gabriel enrolled at Saint-Cyr and I lived at home with my mother and grandmother. I became a good student and built friendships with some of my teachers, especially Abbé Neveu, who taught me philosophy. He was extraordinarily intelligent and open to existential questions. He also took a liking to me. He had a good sense of humor and was immeasurably kind. I remember him lifting his cassock to kick a ball around with us in the playground, and also listening to my confessions while seated together on the steps of the church. Our time there never ended with a list of prayers to recite but instead with a long discussion about man's existence and free will.

My grandmother was subject to all forms of paranoia after Papyrus left us. The Duchesse d'Avoiseul had not greeted her at the end of mass, Baroness Mully had not invited her to her Christmas concert for the first time in her life, Countess Poiteau gave her an odd smile when she met her at a tea hosted by her cousin the Countess de Vilan-court. With my mother this same anxiety transferred itself onto us.

"I beg you, Christiane, to pay close attention to your personal conduct. It's going to be very difficult to find you a husband. So please do everything you can to avoid being repulsive."

"What do you mean repulsive? I've received a lot of attention!"

"That's all we need — for you to be known as an easy girl! Really, that's all we need! Be mindful not to do anything that could be misinterpreted."

"So am I to push boys away or not?"

"Oh, when you pretend you don't get my meaning you are really a pain in the neck!"

One afternoon in March while walking in the streets of Amiens with my mother, I was whistled at by a group of boys who were smoking a cigarette as they watched girls go by. It was a magnificently sunny day on the front edge of spring — the season that boys of that age know belongs to them. I pretended not to notice and looked straight ahead, but it was not enough. My mother stopped in her tracks and said to me, "You cross the street this instant and tell those young men, 'Gentlemen, I am not the person you take me for.'"

"No way, I will not!"

"Christiane! Do you think it's acceptable for it to be said that you're an easy girl?"

"But I've not done anything! Let's go home. We're making a spectacle of ourselves."

"Well, if you won't, I will!"

And so she crossed the street and said what she had to say, while I, red with shame, ran home without waiting for her. When she arrived, her face was lit up with victorious satisfaction. I was determined more than ever to study philosophy in Paris and live at the home of Cousin Vincent's mother, who most certainly would not have exposed me to that kind of humiliation.

When I related such episodes to Gabriel he invariably told me not to get upset and just to accept things without paying so much attention to them. "It's their generation, what do you expect!" was a common refrain.

The Duc d'Avoiseul reigned supreme over our little world of aristocratic rurality. He possessed a large château, a solid, well-documented family tree going back at least five centuries, lots of land, and therefore lots of money. Having lost his wife, with whom he had no children, he had been living in his château with his mother since the age of thirty. Everyone praised this admirable faithfulness to the deceased Duchess.

During the events that I'm about to describe, the Duke was about forty, balding, and showing early signs of a pot-belly; but he was still the dream of every well-born young woman in the area. He hosted a ball that my grandmother did everything in her power to get us invited to. Gabriel, who was on leave in Amiens, was to accompany us. I found the idea amusing because my cousins and brother would be there, but otherwise I was completely uninterested in such distractions. Besides, I was always poorly dressed since we had no money, and my mother and grandmother were constantly criticizing me as too much this or that, or not enough this or that. They forced me to try on an old dress of my mother's that was totally outmoded but that they both declared to be "wonderfully chic!" I was therefore in a very bad mood in the car that brought us to the ball.

"Try to smile, Christiane! Do you realize what it means for you to be invited to the Avoiseuls'? It's a detail that could very well change the attitude that people have toward us and remind them that I am a direct descendant of the Stuarts, and that your grandfather, my deceased husband, was the Count of Louvenciel! The effrontery of your father was a strike against one of the oldest families of France. I am pleased to see that the Duchess has not forgotten our ancestry."

The women in my family were capable in this way of ascending rapidly from a cellar of shame to summits of arrogance.

"Of course, Grandma," I replied distractedly.

Gabriel gave me an arch look to let me know he approved of my bland reaction and then proceeded to imitate the strange hiccup noise that our grandmother always made. His little comedy made me laugh uncontrollably.

"I don't see what's so funny about descending from a family that participated in the Crusades with Saint Louis!"

"I'm not laughing about that, Grandma."

Gabriel continued to hiccup and move his chin like a turkey, which was our grandmother's habit. She couldn't see him from where she was sitting next to my mother in the backseat. My laughing became even louder.

"Well, if you find that funny, perhaps you're not ready to be in the Duchesse d'Avoiseul's salons!"

Gabriel kept on with his hiccuping and head bobbing, and I continued laughing uproariously. Mother scolded us but was powerless to stop us.

All the aristocrats of the region were present as well as a few additional personages such as the prefect and the notary. They all spoke loudly and with the forced gaiety that one is supposed to exhibit on such occasions. Gabriel abandoned me as soon as we arrived and went off with his cousin to check out the young ladies. Grandma Éléonore and my mother seated themselves amid a group of stiff older ladies with sour looks. I hated how I was dressed and wanted to become invisible, especially since I didn't see Laure, my favorite cousin. I approached the buffet table and set about stuffing myself while trying to keep that from being too obvious. Dressed as I was, no one was going to ask me to dance. I had a lace collar that went up to my chin, my dress was too long, and my shoes were simple flats—a real disaster! Other young ladies were displaying their magnificent décolletés and on each of their faces was an easy smile crowning their triumphant juvenile beauty. I sat down at the bottom of a little staircase and watched the party without being seen. But then the Duc d'Avoiseul spotted me and approached.

"You look awfully bored," he said in a kind voice.

"Not in the least! On the contrary, I find it all very amusing. I'm just a little tired," and I blabbered on like that.

It was hard to believe but the Duke was only interested in me. He spent the entire evening with me, tried to get me to dance, and laughed at my attempts at humor. In short, he was discreetly flirting with me, but it did not pass unnoticed, especially by my mother and grandmother, who were absolutely ecstatic.

Thus began my descent into hell.

They were on my case day and night to know if I had received any news, if he had come by, how I had replied, and so on.

At first, like an idiot, by telling of all the Duke's compliments and kind words addressed to me, I was proud to have in a way rehabilitated them in the eyes of the society they were so attached to. It made them so happy that I didn't see any reason to deprive them of that pleasure. They would then speak for hours about what might be the deep motives behind the Duke's taking an interest, since he had not given so much as the time of day to any woman since the death of his wife, and the only answer they could come up with was of course the importance of my lineage, the Crusades, and the kings and queens who circulated in my bloodline — a veritable Capernaum in my veins! I don't mean to brag, but I think the Duke simply had the hots for me.

It was Gabriel who first blew the alarm bell.

"Watch out, sis, or else there'll be no Paris or philosophy for you until the Duke asks for your hand in marriage."

"Stop it, he's twenty years older than me!"

"That's not going to be a problem, neither for him nor for anyone else!"

"But this isn't a livestock auction! I've got a say in this too!"

"Hmm, I don't think so. But really, sis, the Duc d'Avoiseul! You could have hit the ball a little softer."

I started hiding what I was able to hide, but the invitations to the Avoiseul home were always extended to my mother and grandmother as well, and the flowers arrived at the house while I was still at school.

I took my baccalaureate exams and got a particularly good grade on the philosophy test. I was able to celebrate with Abbé Neveu at least—Mother and Grandma Éléonore couldn't have cared less and Gabriel was away doing military training. My grandma did have a costly dress made for me by way of congratulations, but I would have been more appreciative of her gesture if it had been less immediately transparent that she was primping me for the marriage market!

Spring gave way to the oppressive heat of summer. We all missed the fresh breeze of Warvillers, the cry of turtledoves, the bold palette of different shades of green, the whinnying of the horses that we'd comb down at the end of our rides, the smell of the soil, the softness of the lawn under our feet, the tall oaks under which one could read a good book while getting drunk on the scent of freshly cut grass, and then the sunset, which promised with a blinding explosion of red that the next day would be sunny too. Warvillers with its proud windy plains, Warvillers where my little château stood abandoned, uncared for and lifeless.

There being no father to address himself to, the Duke asked my grandmother for my hand in marriage. Grandma, though beside herself with happiness, did not want to reply too hastily. She told him that she'd have to speak with me and that we would give him our answer before the end of the month.

"Good job, Grandma, that gives us two weeks to find words that won't upset him too much."

"What do you mean by that?"

"I mean that he's nice and I don't want to hurt his feelings."

"But of course you're not going to hurt his feelings," interjected my mother. "Why would you do that?"

"Well, no one likes being rejected."

The two old women would have been less surprised if a spaceship had suddenly touched down in the living room.

"You weren't really expecting me to marry that old goat, were you?"

"But Christiane, think a little! You're not going to waste an opportunity like this! Yours is an unbelievable stroke of luck that we simply cannot pass up!"

"It is absolutely, totally, definitively out of the question!"

"Don't speak that way to your mother!" said my grandmother, her cheeks on fire.

"I'm barely eighteen, he's forty—the very idea disgusts me!"

"But what are thinking, you little imp? That you'll have other chances? Do you think that one of the other families we know will allow one of their sons to marry you after what your father did dragging us through the mud?"

"And what about Gabriel? Why aren't you pestering him?"

"Because he's a man. It won't be easy for him either, but maybe he'll be able to make a match with some plain-faced woman."

I can't recall which one of them pronounced which piece of stupidity because for me they had fused into a single, two-headed monster.

That evening I wrote a long letter to Gabriel and the next day I went to call on Abbé Neveu.

"Why don't you ask your aunt Bette for help? Wasn't she helpful with your high school studies? She strikes me as being intelligent and more open than the other women in your family."

"My mother and grandmother can't stand her. And besides, what weight does a rich bourgeoise, and Swiss, have against the Duc d'Avoiseul?"

"My poor child, what are you going to do?"

"If I was of age, I'd run away."

"Oh Lord, no! You must find a solution within your family. What about your uncle Geoffroy?"

"He's my father's brother, you know, and not liked very much either anymore, especially since they suspect that they still see each other."

"Would you like me to speak to their confessor?"

"Whoever they chose as a confessor could not be anyone very accommodating."

"I'm willing to try anything, and you too, you should try to get help from the others in your family."

It was no use. The confessor felt that Abbé Neveu lacked common sense and that an older man was a very good thing for someone like me who needed a firm hand at my young age. He added that it was certainly not their business to meddle in the affairs of these two saintly women.

Aunt Bette and Uncle Geoffroy came to our house, one after the other, to try and persuade my mother and grandmother. They reminded my mother that she had married for love, and that they still remembered her radiant face at the wedding.

"Right, and look how that turned out," said my grandmother, pursing her lips as she always did when she was exasperated.

"But the happiness that comes with love, you mustn't deprive Christiane of that chance!" insisted Aunt Bette.

"We're sparing her great misfortune, you mean to say!"

"Éléonore, I know your rectitude and your sense of duty, but the times really have changed," wailed Aunt Bette.

"Not in our families, my dear. Not in ours. Are you saying you don't remember?"

"Éléonore, I did so love your son, I cannot stand to think that Christiane should never know that kind of happiness."

"Oh, let's stop this sentimental nonsense! The only thing that matters in the end is to stay in one's social milieu and live comfortably with someone who has shared the same upbringing. Everything else is passing fancy and will-o'-the-wisp."

Aunt Bette left with a heavy heart. As for Uncle Geoffroy, he was greeted with mockery: "That the Corbois family parades through my salon dispensing marriage advice, I find that rich indeed!"

My mother was silent. I would like to think she had some reservations about my sacrifice, but she said nothing to confirm that she did.

Gabriel was furious and let it be known, but his declaration only made things worse.

"Unfortunately your children have taken after their father, my poor Marguerite. They are irascible, insolent, and rebellious. We should organize this marriage as quickly as possible if we want to avoid a catastrophe. A father's faults are pardoned in children but not in adults — and especially not when they have the bad taste of resembling him!"

Meanwhile the Duke continued courting me — without ever going beyond any lines of decorum or putting me in an embarrassing situation. He came every day to take tea and invited us regularly to his home. In all I found it more pleasant than to stay trapped with only my mother and grandmother. He brought us in his car and drove us home too. He did everything very slowly — driving, talking, moving, reacting, understanding. I had just turned eighteen and this overall slow speed was to me like being caged in the middle of the desert. At eighteen one moves at a running pace, one is constantly in motion, you only feel good with the wind in your hair.

He was, though, very nice — Mother and Grandma, on the other hand, were odious.

That was why I accepted the marriage in September. I did not do it for them, but because of them. Anything had to be better than life at my grandmother's, and I said to myself that I stood a better chance of persuading the Duke to let me go study in Paris than of persuading my mother and grandmother.

"God protect you, my poor child," said Abbé Neveu.

"You are completely nuts," said Gabriel.

"Christiane, remember that you can change your mind at any time, even at the last minute," said Aunt Bette.

"I'll drive you to city hall, if you like, but are you sure of your decision?" asked Uncle Geoffroy.

"It's the happiest day of my life," said the Duke.

"Finally a rational decision," said Grandma Éléonore.

"My dear, you'll see that all of this is for your own good," said Mother.

"My child, welcome to our family," said the Duchesse d'Avoiseul.

As the day of the wedding approached, the Duc d'Avoiseul became more active. Honestly, I liked him just fine. He was kind, courteous, and considerate. The only problem was that any greater closeness between us I found repugnant. One day he kissed me and I nearly vomited. I found his breath disagreeable, and having his fat fleshy tongue inside my mouth was like being forced to swallow a dirty dishrag. I had already kissed another boy, one of my school friends, and it had been an entirely different experience. I was resigned to getting married, but the idea that it would entail physical intimacy was deeply troubling and literally making me sick. I told myself that I would come up with some solution along the way, that I would lead him into accepting a chaste arrangement, and yet I knew this would not be easy because he clearly found me very attractive.

It was now mid-September and for the occasion we had moved back into the château at Warvillers. My grandmother was willing to undertake any expense—intent as she was that this marriage be a hot topic of conversation throughout the region. So it was, then, that Gabriel and I rediscovered our bedrooms, the great living rooms, and our secret hiding place in the oak tree. The days got shorter. We spent the Friday evening before my wedding drinking a bottle of Pommard and speaking in whispers while seated atop the font where I'd been baptized eighteen years earlier. As it became dark, we did not feel the chill of the evening.

"You are crazy to get married," Gabriel said a bit tipsily.

"You'd do the same if you lived with Mother and Grandma."

"Those two, you'll leave them one day and even have happy memories of each. But marriage — you can't get out of that so easily!"

"Listen, it's decided, so too bad. He's nice."

"I am really blown over by your decision, you know."

"Don't let it upset you, Gabriel. But hey, promise me you won't ever abandon me. You'll come see me often, right? Will you promise me that?"

"Are you ever dumb! Of course I will! You're the person I care most about in the world."

"Yeah, well, you sure hit me enough when we were kids!"

"It was on account of that rat Papyrus."

"You hit me on account of him? Aren't you exaggerating there a little?"

"No, no, no! The hitting came from the bottom of my heart! No, what came from that bastard was your fear that I'd abandon you. But me, I'm different."

"You're like him in everything."

"Wrong. I don't take drugs and I don't abandon people."

"You haven't yet served in two wars and you don't have a piece of shrapnel lodged in your spine."

"You still stick up for him! Incredible! In fact, good for you that you're marrying that old fart, otherwise who knows who you'd bring home!"

It was now late and our hearts were overflowing with half-nostalgic memories — of love received and love given, of the wounds of time and of the fear of everything that we should have released to the blowing wind.

The next day I had a terrible headache and nausea. My mother had me swallow a glass of disgusting salty hot water. I understood from her nervous gestures and sighs that I was not to spoil the party. I should say in her defense that she exhibited no gaiety. She actually looked deeply sad. I believe she thought this was one more part of the cross one had to bear and that now it was my turn to lift and carry that weight. My mother was certain that one did not come into the world to have a lighthearted good time. Grandma Éléonore was not euphoric either. She reminded me of General Kutuzov and his scorched-earth policy, except that instead of sacrificing Moscow to keep it from falling into the hands of Napoleon, it was me she was sacrificing to protect the family's grandeur from the pillory.

They all left for the church and I stayed at the château with Gabriel and Uncle Geoffroy. My bridesmaids were waiting for me at the presbytery with Aunt Elodie, who was in charge of everything. My two companions looked like they were going to a funeral. I tried to ignore them but I had a terrible knot in my stomach. Thus it was that in total silence the car rolled through the gate of our Warvillers home.

The gate closed behind us with a loud metallic clank, swallowing up forever our childhood and with it the only idea we ever had of happiness.

I remained silent, alone with my heaving sighs, which I did my best to keep down.

When Gabriel opened the car door for me, he looked so sad I thought I was going to burst into tears—but then something quite extraordinary happened.

Uncle Geoffroy stood straight as an arrow, his arm slightly bent to accept my own. Gabriel was arranging my train and my veil. Aunt Elodie was on the steps of the church organizing the cortege of children. The families and guests were waiting for me inside.

At that precise moment—I remember it all as though it just happened—I heard a very familiar noise, the *vroom* of Papyrus's motorcycle and sidecar. We all turned to look in the direction of the noise and saw him wearing his leather helmet and big goggles, as in the old days, and approaching at high speed. He pulled up in front of me. We all looked a bit dumbstruck, our jaws hanging open like in cartoons.

"Get in! I forbid you to go through with this."

"But Papyrus, I can't."

"Get in! Now!"

I looked for support from my companions, but they had digested their general surprise and were apparently doing nothing to hold me back.

"Go," said Gabriel. "Go with him!"

"He's right," said Uncle Geoffroy. "Climb on that thing. And as for you, Louis, take care of her this time!"

"Gabriel, Geoffroy—we'll call you tomorrow. Rest easy. Come Christiane, get in, you're not going to let yourself be crucified, are you?"

I pulled off the veil that had belonged to my mother and before her to my grandmother and before her to her mother, and so forth back in time, and I climbed into Papyrus's sidecar.

This caused a big stink. Grandma Éléonore died without pardoning me. Mother took it as the ten thousandth trial she had to undergo to win a good seat in paradise. The people in the region, especially those of our milieu, got sore throats retelling the stories of our family.

I spent the first week with Papyrus in a small hotel in the rue des Saints-Pères, close to where I live now. He explained to me that for all those years he had kept in touch with Aunt Bette, and that she had come to plead with him to do something to prevent the wedding. At first he wanted no part of it. Then on the morning of the wedding day, he said to himself that the shame he'd feel to appear before us all was not enough to justify abandoning me to the dungeon of such a lugubrious fate. When I asked him what exactly his relation with Aunt Bette was, he told me their entire story.

"So why didn't you get married then? To avoid causing Uncle Geoffroy any pain?"

"No doubt."

"But Papyrus, would Bette have gone along with it?"

"Bette thought that the fire at the Goetheanum was an unequivocal sign that what we were doing was horrible and deserved to perish in the fire. And I think she ended up getting me to think the same thing. After that incredible night, she became as elusive as smoke. It was impossible to get her to give any explanation of what she was feeling. She did everything to avoid me, but when circumstances threw us together, her look was always full of tenderness. At least it seemed so to me. When we were back in France,

I waited to know she was alone before trying to see her. She was forced to tell me what her intentions were and she broke my heart. I found her tormented and nervous, but she wouldn't stop repeating that the fire was proof of our damnation and that continuing on in that direction was unpardonable. She said we had to understand the message that had been sent to us and return to being simply the good friends we had been. She caused me so much pain that I told myself I would never again seek any intimacy between us. Losing Bette made me suffer so much that I ended up no longer feeling guilty toward my brother. In the end, he won and his victory canceled my mistake. Over time I got used to the situation, and the devastating feelings I felt for her gradually changed into deep tenderness. That said, I never fell in love again."

"Then why marry Mother?"

"Hey, you were an inch from doing the same thing, I remind you. I was crazy about Bette, so nothing else really mattered. I allowed myself to be carried forward by a sort of inertia. Comfort is all that's left when everything is disenchanted."

After a week, I moved to the home of Cousin Vincent's elderly mother. After Grandma died, I made peace with my mother. She was buried in the little cemetery in Warvillers. Pallbearers were scarce and I know it was my fault. Aunt Bette's hair had gone gray but she still had her magnificent features. I went up to her and gave her a warm hug. "Thank you, Aunt Bette, you saved my life."

Chapter Twenty-Four

Catherine wrote me a long letter in which she tells me that she and Lorenzo are getting along well, even without Luna there to give a direction to their relationship. That's how she put it. She tells me of their tranquillity as they drink the pastis they bought in France while contemplating the Tuscany sunsets. She tells me that she is happy in a way that she never was before.

I am so serene, Mother, that I can even tell you how much I love you. You know it anyway, but you must have suffered to see me irritated by you. I know you. You are so egocentric that nothing that anyone feels about you ever escapes your notice. I always loved you too much, ascribing to you a power that you no longer had, and hating you for leaving me to my fate and letting me become an adult. I lived *my* detachment as *your* abandonment. My childhood was too sweet not to resent you for having to grow up. I send my love and hugs, Mother, and thank you for being all that I criticize, because without that you would be someone different, and I would never want another mother.

Catherine

PS: I ALWAYS give money to musicians in the street.

In September Luna called to tell me she got the top score on her thesis.

"Aunt Bette must be doing somersaults in her grave," I replied, affirming this good news.

"Steiner was a fascinating individual. I enjoyed our meditations on Lucifer, Ahriman, choice, and responsibility. You should have taught philosophy to the workers at Waldorf."

"You're teasing, but I do like that sort of thing."

"Plus, it's thanks to Steiner that I discovered so many things about my family."

"Forget them, my dear, forget them and don't at all believe that they can serve you in any way."

"Really, Grandma, were you making all that up?"

"Absolutely not! Everything I said is completely true."

"I believe you."

She told me that she was going to live in Vancouver, and that her parents were taking it well. She thought they seemed good together. It appears Catherine has been laughing. What I would pay to see her laugh. Before hanging up, I promised Luna that I would spend Christmas with them. I then went into my husband's office to get a whiff of the scent of his tobacco when all of a sudden I was overcome with remorse. I called Luna back.

"My dear, there is one thing in what I told you that I invented."

"Oh, that's too bad. What?"

"Papyrus did drive off on his motorcycle and sidecar, but he came to pick me up at the church in an old Peugeot. I thought saying I jumped in the sidecar was more dashing, don't you agree?"

"I totally agree. A sidecar is way cooler! We'll keep that version."

We hung up. The moon was beginning its milky ascent into the drab gray Parisian sky. Place Saint-Sulpice was slowly emptying. People were going home and the newspaper kiosk was closing for the night.

I lay down on my bed and closed my eyes.

Chapter Twenty-Five

I will climb up onto the rock my husband and father-in-law used to jump from into the Channel, careful not to injure my feet on any sharp mussel or barnacle shell. There will be oyster shells that the tide will have left on our reef. I will fill my lungs with spray, and while the gulls are defending the sky with menacing cries, I will dive into the freezing water.

I will swim as far as the Gulf of Dinard. I will then head west and go beyond the lights of Saint-Malo. I will swim in the direction of Dover on the coast of England.

I will swim without ever stopping.

I will reach the ocean.

I will swim and swim and swim.

I will swim until the devil takes me.

Acknowledgments

To write a book is a very solitary journey. You must be left alone with your own story and imagination, and find the courage to dig into your inner feelings to be sincere and credible. That is what happens in the first stage of this labor. Then you have to cope with the other stages. It's always extremely delicate to expose yourself to criticism and accept that you could not please everyone. That is when your publisher becomes incredibly important. I want to thank, first of all, my friend Judith Gurewich, for being so clever, honest, and supportive. Thanks to Christopher Jon Delogu, who did a remarkably faithful translation. Also, my gratitude to all the Other Press team for their time, their intelligence, and the happy moments spent together.